CALLOUS PRINCE

BECKER GRAY

D1519956

CHAPTER ONE

SLOANE

I CHANGED MY mind the minute I saw the ballroom.

"No," I said, coming to a halt. "No, I think I'd rather not."

"Come on," Serafina van Doren wheedled. "We've been planning this for weeks. *Pleeeease.*"

"No, *you've* been planning this for weeks," I corrected. "*I've* been dreading this."

Through the doors, the entire student population of Pembroke Preparatory Academy was arrayed in a glittering panoply of wealth and privilege—silk gowns, elaborate masks, jewelry borrowed from Mommy or Grandmama—the works.

The ballroom itself had also been spared no expense. There were flickering candelabras everywhere, and garlands of greenery threaded through with autumn leaves and berries. Entire trees with leaves the color of flames had been brought in, along with green-leafed vines hung with hefty pumpkins. The cumulative effect was to make the ballroom feel like an enchanted autumn forest—perfect for this year's Halloween masquerade theme.

Fairyland.

The annual Pembroke Halloween Masquerade was one of the events that Serafina lived for—and one that I'd managed to successfully avoid for the last three years. I wasn't really all that much for dressing up. Or being on display. Or being around people in general, actually.

I much preferred to hang back, to watch from the shadows unobserved, to escape notice. It would be essential if I wanted to follow in my father's clandestine footsteps, but that wasn't the only reason I did it.

The other reason I hid in the shadows would certainly be here tonight, watching the ballroom with disdain pulling at his beautiful, sullen mouth, candlelight flickering off his white hair and his eerily golden eyes.

He was the same reason I was regretting letting Serafina talk me into this. *Last chance*, my ass. What did I care that this was my senior year and my last chance to go to the masquerade? All I wanted was to be free of Pembroke—I certainly wasn't going to be pining after a dumb costume party when I was carving through the world's chaos and mayhem at INTERPOL.

"Look, you're already dressed for it," Sera coaxed. "Why not come in and at least give your costume a chance to be seen?"

I rarely felt self-conscious, but seeing the ballroom packed with silk and velvet and lace made me balk. "No one wants to see this costume," I muttered.

"Uh-uh. I think it's crazy hot," Aurora declared. She plucked at the half cape I wore over one shoulder. "You look like a 16th century fairy assassin. Who *fucks*."

Fairy assassin who fucks had indeed been the theme of the costume—Serafina's theme, not mine. All I'd asked for was a costume with pants and boots. And maybe a sword.

Serafina had come back with skin-tight black pants and knee-high black boots, an ornately handled rapier for my hip, and a velvet capelet which matched the light jade of my eyes and set off my lingering summer tan. And of course, the tight black corset that went over the white Renaissance-era blouse. "Sera, do you want to explain to me why I was your unfortunate guinea pig and not Tannith?"

Sera planted a kiss on my cheek. "Because, my love, Tannith is currently in Los Angeles for the fellowship, and she needed to focus."

"Like you couldn't have flown her in for this."

She grinned. "I could have. But you were the far more fun project."

Before we'd come here tonight, she'd dressed me, slicked my short bob back, and fastened a mask over my face that matched my cape. "There," she'd said proudly. "You look like you just finished fucking some gorgeous but dissolute prince and now you're creeping through the palace to kill his father. Tannith would absolutely *die* if she saw this."

Tannith was our resident bookworm—well, *usually* our resident bookworm. She was currently doing a fellowship in Los Angeles and had been gone all semester. We missed her an awful lot, and I especially missed her right now, when I needed an anchor in the storm that was Sera and Aurora in full Party Mode.

But in the end, I'd liked the idea of the fairy assassin who fucks enough that I'd let Sera and Aurora pack me in the van Doren limo and drag me all the way to the ballroom doors before my doubts crashed in again.

"I don't know," I said in the here and now. "I think I'll just head back. You two don't need me—"

"Is this about my brother?" Aurora asked. She let go of my cape so she could touch my elbow, and underneath her pearl-studded mask, I could see her golden eyes go soft with concern. The same golden eyes that belonged to her twin brother.

Lennox.

Lennox Lincoln-Ward. A literal, actual prince. The most beautiful boy I'd ever seen.

And also the worst. The meanest and the most heartless. Callous beyond belief.

Aurora's voice suddenly went bright and helpful. "I could kill him for you, you know."

I gave a small laugh. "I think that's my line."

Sera crossed her arms, studying the ballroom. She had that look on her face—the one I thought of as the Queen look. Like she'd just ridden up to a battlefield on her steed and was about to order the cannons to fire. Her thick curls were pinned in an elaborate updo and set with flashing red gems, and her scarlet gown brought out the jewel tones in her medium-brown skin. Aurora and Lennox might have been actual royalty, but Sera was every inch Pembroke's real monarch tonight.

"He doesn't get to do this," Sera said, eyes on the ostentatious revelry in front of her. "He doesn't get to keep you away from things you want to do."

I opened my mouth to protest that I didn't actually want to do this, but then I closed it again as her words truly sank into my mind. She was right, as a queen usually was. It was stupid to let Lennox chase me away from anything. Despite the fact that he was Liechtensteiner royalty and part of the Hellfire Club—and despite his persistent hatred and low-key torture of me—this was my damn school too. I deserved to be at this silly ball just as much as he did, and I was done with this pointless game of ours. The Fairy Assassin Who Fucks was going to dance, drink, and laugh like she never had before, just to spite him.

For three years, Lennox Lincoln-Ward had tried to make my life a living hell.

And tonight, that ended for good.

AN HOUR LATER, I was less sure.

I'd thought it would be as simple as ignoring Lennox; I thought I'd barely notice he was here.

But I hadn't taken two things into account.

Firstly—there was no such thing as me *ignoring* Lennox, and there hadn't been since the first week of freshman year when he started persecuting me for no reason at all.

His mere presence made me flare with awareness and trepidation; simply knowing he was in the room made my skin tighten and my pulse race. Tonight was no exception, and as I tried to laugh with my friends, as I accepted a few dances from boys I barely knew, I could feel his eyes on me, burning into my skin. Whenever I looked his way, he was already looking somewhere else, but I *knew* he was watching me. Hating me. It made me tense, electric. Like I was about to spar with my martial arts instructor—certain I was going to lose but eager to prove myself all the same.

Secondly—I had not adequately prepared myself for how Lennox would look tonight. It honestly hadn't occurred to me that he could be any more devastatingly beautiful than he was in everyday life, but here he was, putting everyone else to shame. His starkly blond hair tumbled white and silky around a circlet of golden stars set into his hair, and the crown only further set off the sharp gold of his eyes. The white mask he wore left his forehead, jaw, and mouth bare, and rather than disguise the near-inhuman elegance of his pale features, the mask only served to highlight them.

The jaw so gorgeously sharp that it looked rendered by an artist. A mouth so painfully sensual, even when pulled into its usual sulky pout.

And his costume . . .

While most of the Pembroke guys had used the masquerade as an excuse to show off their latest bespoke suits and imported Italian shoes, Lennox had taken the fairyland theme to heart and come fully as a fairy prince. He was barefoot and wearing tight leather pants, with a Renaissance-style white shirt and a doublet made of gold silk and velvet. Both the doublet and the shirt were open—and the shirt was all the way unlaced, exposing a shocking amount of smooth, firm skin. The hollow of his collarbone, the lean but solid muscles of his chest—they were all on display.

He really looked like he had just strolled out of a fairy forest. He looked wicked and unearthly.

He looked perfect.

It wasn't fair.

It wasn't fair that he hated me, when I'd done nothing to deserve it. It wasn't fair that he looked handsome and delicious while I looked—well, less like an assassin who fucks and more like a girl who was uncomfortable wearing dresses and lipstick.

After I finished dancing with a boy from my AP Physics class, I went for a drink of water. There was stronger stuff on hand if I wanted it, not to mention all sorts of artisanal punches that were all fairyland-themed, but I wanted to keep my head and stay hydrated. A hydrated body is a strong body, and a flexible one too, and I needed my body to be both.

I took my water behind a tree and watched the dancers from underneath its arching branches. I watched *him*, dancing with a girl a year or two younger than us. Whatever she said made him laugh; it made a smile carve itself across his normally-sulky mouth.

And as always, whenever he smiled, there was an answering slice across my heart.

"I've seen lions less aware of wounded gazelles than Lennox is of you tonight," a silky voice said from behind me.

I turned to see the devil himself, Rhys Huntington, standing just behind my shoulder, pale, dark-haired, and dressed all in black: a black suit that probably cost as much as a regular person's car, black and silver vest underneath, black silk tie stuck through with a ruby-studded tie pin.

"Lennox doesn't even know I'm alive," I responded evenly, knowing it was a lie but also too wary to engage Rhys further. "And I thought tonight's theme was fairyland—not vampire coven."

Rhys stepped forward, a tilt to his sharp-edged mouth. We were shoulder to shoulder now. "I'm a dark fairy. From the Unseelie Court. Don't you know your fairy stories?"

The honest answer was no. As the only daughter of an INTERPOL bureau chief, my childhood had often been stranger than any fairy tale, and anyway, my father wasn't much for fantasy. He was all about what could be seen and touched and uncovered—all about this world and those who would sin against it. I suppose I took after him in that way.

If only there wasn't a certain sinner that fascinated me so much . . .

"Anyway," Rhys pronounced, still in that silky voice, "if you don't think Lennox is looking at you tonight, just watch this."

Within the blink of an eye, my water was set on a table and I was whisked out onto the dance floor. *In Rhys's arms.* Staring up at those near-black eyes glittering from behind his dark mask.

"What are we doing?" I asked him, easily catching the rhythm of the waltz as he turned me across the floor. I was a decent dancer. It wasn't so different than martial arts, after all: posture, form, balance. And Rhys was a surprisingly graceful partner for being someone whom I'd always assumed was pure evil.

Whenever we turned, my cape swung out behind me, and whenever we stepped, Rhys's firm hand on my back made sure to keep my hips close to his. For anyone watching, the dance might have looked . . . romantic.

"I would've thought it was obvious what we're doing, Sloane Lauder," Rhys said softly. "I'm proving a point about Lennox."

My father had trained me better, he really had, but when it came to Lennox, I never could seem to control myself. I swiveled my head and looked to where I'd seen him last.

And was hit with a golden gaze so malevolent I could practically feel its heat all the way out here in the middle of the dance floor.

"He *is* watching," I said, more to myself than to the tall devil spinning me around.

"He's always watching you."

"He hates me, you know."

Rhys smiled a cipher-like smile. "Maybe."

"I don't think he likes seeing me have fun."

The cipher-like smile grew bigger. "If he hates you dancing, then he'll definitely hate this."

And right there, right in the middle of the ballroom floor with couples waltzing around us and candles flickering everywhere, Rhys Huntington kissed me.

Kissed me!

I could have fended him off if I wanted. No one could touch me when I didn't want to be touched, thanks to my father and years of martial arts. But I found . . . I found I didn't want to.

Not at first, at least.

His kiss was silky, just like his voice, and his mouth was surprisingly warm for someone with a heart chiseled from ice. And while it didn't necessarily set my heart to racing the same way a mere glance from Lennox did, and while it didn't make me hot and restless the way the mere thought of Lennox's mouth made me, the kiss wasn't *un*pleasant. It was almost nice, in fact. Like the sensation of kissing without all the fervor and heat that usually accompanied the act. Like the *idea* of kissing without all the complicated feelings coming to mess it up.

Rhys's fingers curled around my cape as he pulled me closer and deepened the kiss, his tongue slipping between my lips to caress mine. It was instinct as much as anything that had me tilting my face up to offer Rhys more—and that's when I heard it.

The clatter and crash of a candelabra falling over, and the gasps and shrieks that followed. I broke away from Rhys's kiss to see Lennox disappearing through the far doors, his stride quick and furious.

From the way people were staring and whispering, it was clear he was the one who knocked over the candelabra.

As if he'd flung it to the ground in anger before storming away.

"Well, then," Rhys said with satisfaction, his eyes also on Lennox's retreating form. "I was right."

CHAPTER TWO

LENNOX

*R*AGE. IT WAS the only way to explain what was happening to my body. My skin was clammy and hot. And all I wanted to do was hit something. It was like my skin hummed and my blood was trying to force its way out by exploding it.

I was going to kill him. Bloody Rhys.

I knew the Hellfire Club wasn't a knitting circle or an etiquette class. We mostly did whatever the fuck we wanted—hell, the whole purpose of the club was so the wealthy and the powerful could increase their wealth and power so that they could continue to do whatever the fuck they wanted after they left Pembroke. This kind of power-brokering, good old boys club shit didn't exactly make for a milieu of politeness and courtesy. We were sharks chosen by the sharks who came before us, and when we graduated, we would wade into an ocean where we were already kings.

So no, we were no knitting circle, but there were still a few fucking *codes*.

You didn't fuck with other Hellfire members, and you certainly didn't fuck with their toys.

I knew better than to totally lose my shit at the masquerade ball though. I'd been raised better than that. There were appropriate times and places for caving to anger, and the ball wasn't it. Besides, there was no way any adult in there would have let me kick Rhys's arse the way I'd wanted to. Also, I wanted to give him more time to sober up. Because when I put him into the ground, I wanted him to remember it. I wanted him to feel it. I wanted to burn him down.

Some fucking mate he was.

She was mine. She had *always* been mine. And Rhys, arsehole that he was, thought he could just stroll in and take her from me? No. Ever since I laid eyes on hers, we'd had our unwritten rule. She was *mine* to torment. Mine to *torture*.

After what her father had done to mine, it was the payback I needed. She was nobody else's to even look at. And all things being even, Rhys didn't even want her, I was certain of it. He just found her interesting for some fucking reason.

All around me, limousines dropped off the children of the world's wealthiest at the Everwood Country Club, this year's location for the Halloween Masquerade Ball. Nestled along a lake, surrounded by the jaw-dropping fall foliage, the country club was the perfect location. The employees had set lights into the water along the property to carry on the fairyland theme.

Knowing I'd be drinking, I'd opted for the safer option of the limo. Some of the other lads had caught a ride with Owen.

I wanted to leave, just say fuck it all and head back to campus, but Keaton was riding with me, so I had to wait. I was in the middle of texting him when I saw Owen and Rhys coming my way.

Owen, as to be expected, was in cold control. If he'd been in the mood to display any emotions, he'd likely be disapproving of my antics inside the ballroom. Owen was our living and breathing Ice King. He didn't fucking get it. He had no feelings. Or he'd been smart and learned a long time ago to lock that shit away.

Just seeing Rhys's face again made me want to raze every car on the jammed country club drive. He gave me nothing. He was always a cool and contained sociopath. "What the fuck, Rhys?"

He gave me his barely-there smile, those cruel eyes crinkling at the corners, telling me that he'd been looking forward to this. "What the fuck what?"

"That kiss, that fucking show—what the hell is wrong with you?"

He grinned then, and it was so strange to see a full-on smile on his face, I almost didn't know what to do.

You kick his arse, that's what you do.

I re-focused myself. "You're such a piece of shit. You don't even want her."

"But I *do* want her. She's interesting to me."

Owen could see where this was going, and his lips pressed into a harsh line as he stepped between us. "Lads, get your shit under control. This isn't the place to do this. Teachers are milling about. You two tossers want to take a hunk out of each other's hides, you do it where it can't be seen. And where you won't get blood on my tux."

"Careful, Mr. Robot, somebody will begin to think you care."

He lifted a dark brow. "Hardly, I'm just calculating the odds of who to bet on in this fight. I'm inclined to put my money on Rhys, because he's not whining like a bitch."

"Fuck you. And for the record, I have exactly zero fucks to give about teachers." What, like they were going to expel me? I was fucking royalty.

You are also the son of royalty. This is what's expected of you.

I knew what I needed to do, but unfortunately, I couldn't stamp down the fury.

Rhys was laughing now. What the hell was he saying?

"I have to tell you, Lennox, I'm amused by your response. I thought you *hated* her."

"I do. The point is, she is *mine*."

Rhys's eyes went wide. "She's yours?" Mirth laced each of his words.

"Yes, that's right. Mine to torture. Mine to ignore. Mine to pull along on a string like a puppet. *Mine*," I ground out. Her father had ruined my life. Systematically. Everything was gone because of her family. And so, if I was going to take my revenge, it was going to be through her. And Rhys wasn't going to ruin her before I got there.

"Did you tell her that? Does she know she's—" he made air quotes. "*Yours?*"

I lunged for him again, and this time, Owen put a hand on my chest, more than capable of stopping me. We were about the same height, but

I was leaner. He had a good twenty pounds of muscle over me, but I was meaner. I spun out from him, elbowed him in the chest for good measure so he'd back off, and Rhys just taunted me, "If you want her, you are more than welcome to try and take her from me. But I'm not going to just give her to you. I think I'll play with her for a while. You know, she's surprisingly a good kisser. Soft lips. The way her tongue tentatively seeks yours out as if she can't believe her luck. God. I always find that a major turn on. These quiet girls, they're the best ones in bed. It's going to be fun finding out with Sloane."

I lunged at him again. This time, Owen had an arm around my waist, and out of the corner of my eye, I saw Keaton running towards us too. Fuck. Not Keaton. He was building up for the pro rugby season. *Shit.*

"Guys, what's going on? You don't want to do this out in full view."

Rhys grinned. "Hey, I'm a lover, not a fighter. I prefer to destroy people without my hands, but if it comes down to it, I will use them."

It was true. Rhys never needed to lift a finger. The guy was always working out though. Fucking *Muay Thai* or whatever it was that he did all the time. He had his trainer personally come to the school. Who the hell did that? But despite being probably more than capable of using his fists, Rhys was mean as a snake. He preferred to destroy you with words.

So beat him at his own game.

"You can let me go. I'm not going to fucking hit him." Lies. All lies.

Keaton laughed. "I love you, man, but I don't believe you."

"Rhys, you know what, you can have your fun with Sloane. It's all right. I get it. You're bored, but you'll get tired of her too."

He grinned. "I don't know if I will. You know, she's fascinating. Smart as a whip. Slightly deadly. And she's unusual. God, those lips. I mean, it must kill you that you've never tapped that at all, because wow, the girl can kiss."

It felt like there was a dragon in my chest trying to claw its way out.

Be smart. Use his one weakness against him.

I forced myself to still then. "You know what, you're right. You can get whoever you want. And yes, I'm losing my shit. I don't like someone stealing my toys. But you do have a point. We're all free agents here, except for Keaton, and that's by choice. But we should think outside the box, explore opportunities we've never considered before. You know, Sera was looking damn fine tonight. Well fit. Gorgeous, really. But that red dress, her mask, the hood, she looked like something from Venice. I think I'll find out just what she had on under those skirts, yeah?"

I found out in those two seconds exactly what happens when you poke a dragon. I'd miscalculated. And unfortunately, I was the only one being held back by our friends.

Rhys was quicker than a flash. It was almost like the motherfucker flew into the air, and he was on me. His first hit grazed just off my jaw because I turned to go with it.

When the rest of my mates realized they were holding the wrong arsehole, they tried to go for him, but he was quicker.

I'm not proud of it, but I did give him a good sucker punch to the kidney. But Rhys really was the devil. He didn't cry out. He didn't moan. But he did hiss and turn on me, his hands knotted into tight fists, but this time, Keaton had him. He'd hooked Rhys's arm and wrapped it around his back. Owen planted himself in front of him, like a statue made of ice. Both of them were muttering something in low tones.

Now free, I stood at my full height and grinned. "Yeah, everyone knows how hot Sera is.

Now I'm going to find out just what she tastes like."

Rhys snarled at me. "If you put your fucking hands on her, I will *kill* you."

Being the arsehole that I was, I grinned back. "Oh, but I thought Sloane was the most interesting person to you. I guess not. I think I'll go find Sera now and see what she's up to." Then I deliberately turned and stalked away.

It was a calculated risk. He could have lunged for me. We were too evenly built, so it would have been one hell of a fight. But I was confident that Keaton and Owen had him. So I continued on my way, and I didn't turn back.

I'd considered Rhys a friend, but he'd stepped over the line, and I was going to make him pay for it.

CHAPTER THREE

SLOANE

"THANK YOU," THE junior said gratefully. She looked around the empty classroom, as if to confirm again that we were alone. "You're sure it's gone?"

I uncrossed my arms and gave her a sympathetic but utilitarian nod. "He had it in his photo library, and he'd emailed it to himself, but he hadn't sent it to anyone else yet. Both the phone and the email have been scrubbed, along with his cloud storage."

The junior slumped in relief. "Thank god," she murmured. "Thank god."

Her asshole ex had threatened to send a nude picture of her to everyone at the school once he found out she was dating a new boyfriend. I took care of it last night, using some stealth and a few sturdy lockpicking tools.

"I'm so glad I came to you," she said. "Do I . . . like . . . owe you anything?"

I shook my head. "Free of charge."

She squinted at me. "Are you like Pembroke's revenge porn vigilante or something?"

The corners of my mouth pulled up. I liked the idea of being a resident vigilante, but really I just had a keen sense of justice, and—much like Liam Neeson—a very particular set of skills. Over the last two or three years, I'd become something of a Veronica Mars here at school, helping students out when the administration couldn't. It was unbelievable the amount of boys who thought sending a girl's nudes around was a totally justified thing to do, but I also had my share of "is he or she cheating?" cases and a fair amount of theft. It kept me from getting bored, kept me sharp and proficient at moving through the shadows, and also it was just fun. Satisfying.

Some students had sports, some had parties— I had this.

"I'm just happy I could help," I told her.

"Me too," she said. "Thank you again."

I nodded and made for the door.

"Hey, do you know anybody at Croft Wells who does what you do?" she asked.

Croft Wells was another coed prep school

only an hour away, and Pembroke's eternal rival. Despite that, there were still a healthy amount of cross-school friendships and even dating. "I don't," I said. "Why?"

The junior sighed. "My cousin says there's been some girls attacked at parties over there, and they don't know if it's like one guy or a bunch of guys or what. The police and campus admin have been no help. Seems like the kind of thing you'd be good at."

I frowned at that. "When was the last assault?"

She shook her head. "They stopped in the spring. Maybe the attacker got bored?"

Or he found a new hunting ground.

But I didn't tell the junior that. "Probably he got bored," I said reassuringly, and then I stepped through the door and made my way to class, vowing to keep an eye on things here at Pembroke.

I had no way to get to Croft Wells, but I'd be good and goddamned before I let an asshole get away with that here at Pembroke.

"RHYS IS LOOKING at you," Sera announced a few hours later.

Even in the clanking, chattering din of Pembroke's giant, vaulted dining hall, I could hear something strained in her voice. I glanced up from my dog-eared copy of *The Book of Five Rings* and gave her a quelling look. "Stop it. You know I don't care."

"You certainly seemed like you cared at the masquerade a couple days ago," she pointed out.

"It was just a kiss," I said, going back to my Musashi. "It wasn't a big deal."

"For 'not a big deal', my brother went totally off his trolley," Aurora said cheerfully. "And Rhys is still looking, by the way."

For the millionth time, I wished Tannith were here instead of spending the semester in Los Angeles. Because normally we absconded to the library together to read during lunch, and so it never mattered what Rhys Huntington was or was not doing.

To satisfy my friends—and *not* because I cared that a certain gold-eyed prince might also be sitting there—I looked over at the Hellfire Club's table across the hall. They sat at the far end of the wood-ceilinged, portrait-bedecked space, right under the largest stained glass window in the room. A cluster of gorgeous, insolent boys, sprawled in their chairs like so many bored lions. The bright autumn sunlight through the glass lit their table with shafts of blazing orange and glowing ruby—as if hellfire truly burned in the air around them.

Fitting, since next to Lennox sat the devil himself, grinning at me from across the room like we shared some kind of secret. I ducked my head as soon as I realized we'd met eyes, but it was too late, of course. Rhys had obviously been waiting for just this moment.

"Rhys is standing up," Sera said, her voice still strange. "He's walking over here."

"Oh, Lennox looks quite tetchy now," Aurora said, sounding pleased. She took typical sisterly delight in anything that annoyed her twin. "Yes, very tetchy indeed."

I couldn't help it; I lifted my head again, my eyes sliding right past Rhys's approaching form to Lennox again. Even at this distance, I could see the hatred sizzling in his eyes and the angry tilt to his mouth. The same look he'd leveled my way since that first day in freshman seminar.

I'd long since stopped trying to understand why Lennox Lincoln-Ward hated me—although I used to think about it constantly, used to wonder if I could fix whatever it was. Or at least change it so that he'd *stop*. It couldn't be that I'd offended him before the first day of freshman year, because until then I'd gone to school in D.C. And it couldn't have been anything I'd done that morning, because when I initially walked into the seminar, he'd looked up at me and offered me a careless grin—like he wanted to know what my lip gloss tasted like but he was too lazy to try to find out.

It wasn't until he heard my name that he'd swiveled his head to stare at me—lips parted in shock, eyes bright with fury—and then abruptly scooped up his bag and stormed out of the room.

And after that, the true torment began.

Lube in my book bag, caricatures drawn of me in bathrooms, classroom projects replaced with a single, thoroughly dead rose. The rumors he started about me—some silly, some ridiculous, some vicious as hell—and his cruel laughter following me everywhere I went.

And his *presence*.

The presence of him was its own torture.

He didn't stalk me, I wouldn't go that far, but he haunted me, he encircled me and bedeviled me, made it so that every corner of Pembroke was suffused and pervaded with him. He would be in doorways I needed to go through, blocking my escape, or sitting at my desk before class started, eating an apple and staring at me with glittering eyes. He'd be at my chair in the library when I'd come back from grabbing a book, his three-thousand-dollar Italian shoes kicked up on the table, or jogging behind me as I did my morning run on the track, never approaching me or coming closer, but keeping pace with me perfectly no matter how much I sped up or slowed down.

Being raised by my father meant that I was more capable of defending myself than anyone knew, and it also meant I wasn't in the habit of taking anyone's shit. For every time I found my books and tablet slicked in lube, I discreetly and efficiently picked the lock to his room and replaced his hair gel with KY and his toothpaste with Astroglide (for variety). I wasn't a fan of bathroom vandalism, but I did help myself to some classified student records early on, and then occasionally amused myself by distributing his cell phone number to giggling freshmen eager to kiss a real-life prince.

And when he blocked a doorway, when he sat at my desk, when he ran behind me every morning with a gray hood drawn over his striking blond hair—I never let him see the fear that sizzled over my skin. I couldn't.

Because if he saw the fear, then he might see how it mingled with other feelings. How the adrenaline made my blood spark and made something deep in my core go all twisty and hot.

He could never know.

I could survive his hatred maybe, but his pity?

His smug superiority once he learned that under my defiance crawled something much, much more embarrassing than fear?

I didn't even think I could *attempt* to endure that. I would have to move and change my name. I would have to change all distinguishable identifiers. I would have to dye my hair and wear colored contacts and take the helix piercing out of my upper ear. And I really liked that piercing.

No, he could never know.

Which actually made it very convenient that Rhys was coming over to our table just now. Although he'd been as bad to me as Lennox had over the years—I suspected the most creatively depraved of the bathroom graffiti was the work of Rhys's degenerate mind—I really hadn't minded kissing him at the masquerade. And I minded even less that it made me appear indifferent to Lennox, that it made it *very clear* I did not think about Lennox in any kind of kissing capacity ever—that I did not sometimes let my hand wander over my body at the thought of Lennox's mouth or his lean body or his elegant, long-fingered hands which looked like they'd feel so very good shoved into my panties.

Rhys was an opportunity to protect myself, and I'd learned early on from my father never to waste those.

My father.

I had wondered before . . .

Well, there *had* been a scandal with Lennox and Aurora's father, years ago—a massive Ponzi scheme and substantial prison time after. INTERPOL had been the investigating agency, and it had been the US and several European bureaus working together to make the arrest. I'd asked my father about it once, not long after Lennox's torment had begun, but he told me he had only consulted on the case once and barely looked at it after. So I knew his vendetta couldn't be about my father.

Maybe Lennox merely hated anyone or any-thing to do with INTERPOL? But Aurora had mentioned more than once that both she and Lennox were very happy about their father being in prison and hoped he'd stay there, so it made no sense to hate me over a father whom they were quite satisfied to have rotting in prison.

It couldn't be that. So what was it?

"Ladies," Rhys was saying as he sauntered

over. "How beautiful you all look today."

"We're not interested," Sera replied shortly. "Fuck off."

The evil grin faded, replaced by a look so cold that even I fought the urge to shiver.

Sera, for her part, just continued glaring up at him.

"I'm not here for you," Rhys said in a silky voice.

"Then god is real," said Sera.

Rhys's face didn't change, but his eyes did, growing even blacker. "If I want you, I'll have you."

Sera looked away, her expression cool. "I'd like to see you try."

And then—most frightening of all—Rhys smiled. "Maybe one day, van Doren. But only after you beg, and who knows? Maybe then it will be too late."

Sera rolled her eyes and got up to leave. Rhys stepped forward, towering over my slender friend, and for a moment, I thought he might stop her from leaving. But then, with that eerie smile again, he stepped aside, and with a huff, Sera stalked away from the table with a muttered *see you later* to me and Aurora.

Rhys took her seat with a prompt grace which

suggested he'd been planning on driving her off all along. "Now, Sloane," he said, as if we were picking up on a conversation we'd started before. "What time should I have you picked up next Saturday for the gala?"

Aurora nearly spit out her drink. "You're going to the Huntington Gala together?"

"No," I said, narrowing my eyes at Rhys. "I've never been invited to the gala, remember, Aurora?" While my father made decent money in his work—decent enough to send me here—he didn't make *gala* money, and I hadn't exactly grown up with the gala set. The annual Huntington bash was one of the events that everybody knew about and only a chosen, insanely wealthy few could attend. And I had never been one of them.

Which I truly hadn't minded—Tannith was as unconnected and socially obscure as me, and so we usually spent the evening in the near-empty common room watching a weird mix of BBC literary adaptions (her choice) and bloody action movies (mine). And I hated getting dressed up anyway.

Plus, the Huntington mansion was outside of Boston, which meant that attending the gala was a weekend-long commitment with the long-ass drive factored in. No thanks.

"Consider this your invitation then," Rhys said, undaunted. "And of course, you're welcome to come down early with me on Friday. Spend the night, see my childhood room."

Even out of the corner of my eye, I could see Aurora's jaw drop.

"Okay, this is getting weird. I'm out," I said, standing up and slinging my bag over my chest. "I'll see you later, Aurora. Bye, Rhys."

Rhys was up and next to me in an instant.

"Let me walk you to your next class," he said smoothly, taking my hand in his.

Just like his kiss at the masquerade, it didn't feel unpleasant at all. It was nice, actually. I normally didn't mind that karate and exercise kept my curves more flat than interesting, and I had no interest in changing how I dressed— usually a short ponytail and boots to go with my school uniform. But I couldn't deny that I was hardly luring boys to my side this way and getting to hold hands with someone was a nice change. Even more so when he pulled me out into the almost empty corridor connecting the dining hall to the main lecture building and pressed his warm lips to mine.

"Come to my family's gala," he murmured,

pulling back to look down at me. Those black eyes were inscrutable. I had no idea what he was thinking and no reason to trust that it might be good.

"Wouldn't you rather go with someone else?" I asked. "*Anyone* else?" I wasn't a knockout like Sera or royalty like Aurora. I wasn't rich like Clara Blair and her friends. The most interesting things about me—what my father did for a living and all the things he'd taught me—weren't apparent on the surface.

In short, there was no reason to believe that Rhys wasn't playing some kind of stupid Hellfire joke on me right now. But then he said the one thing that made me believe him.

"I'm never going to fall in love with you, Sloane Lauder. But right now, you're the most interesting girl at this school to me. And I like interesting things." He gave me an assessing look, like he could see my bra and panties underneath my school blazer and skirt. "I like interesting things quite a lot."

With another penetrating but mysterious look, he walked away, calling over his shoulder, "Five p.m. next Friday, Sloane. We're going to my house."

I didn't answer him. Mostly because he was

already prowling away, but also because the answer that leapt to my lips wasn't an immediate *no*. As much as I thought I'd hate the idea of going to something like the Huntington Gala . . . it *was* really flattering to be asked.

Maybe it wouldn't be the worst thing if I went.

With a glance down at my phone, I saw I had some time before my next class, and I decided to take the long way to the science building. I'd only made it a handful of steps down the stone-flagged corridor when the hair prickled on the back of my neck.

I spun around just in time to stop Lennox from grabbing my arm, my training flaring up instinctively. I blocked his grab and was about to seize his wrist and twist it when he did something I had no preparation for.

He hauled me tight against him with his free arm around my back, so tight that I could feel the angry heave of his chest and the firm wall of his abdomen, and at the press of his body against mine, all my instincts left me. Well, all except the dumbest one, which pleaded for me to rub against him like a cat and purr until he petted me.

"No need to fly into a fit, darling," Lennox said, his British accent curling around me like the

CALLOUS PRINCE

tendrils of a lovely but lethal frost. "We can be civilized about this."

"Civilized about wha—*Lennox!*" He was dragging me into a nearby storage closet, throwing open the door with one hand as he easily pulled me inside. The only way I could have broken free was by hurting him—a finger rake to his eagle-gold eyes, a knee to the groin, maybe some broken fingers—and I found . . . well, I found that I didn't really want to do that. Not until I had no other choice, at least.

"Let. Me. Go," I demanded the minute the door was closed.

He flicked on a light, still keeping me close, and then looked down at me. We were surrounded by boxes of paper towels and industrial-sized rolls of toilet paper, but even in here, he looked like a prince; arrogant and majestic. The dim light from the single light bulb caressed his sharp cheekbones and pout-shaped mouth.

"Lennox," I bit out. "I'm not asking. Let me go."

He looked a little surprised at himself when he admitted, "But I don't want to."

I glared up at him. "You realize I can make you, right? And it won't be pleasant."

"I don't doubt it," he said honestly. "But I

37

don't think you want to make me. I think you like being right here." A cruel smirk twisted the corner of his mouth. "I *definitely* like you being right here."

He tugged me even closer—and I could feel more than his chest and stomach now, I could feel his . . . oh wow.

Wow, wow, wow.

He might technically be a prince, but there was one place where he was *all* king.

No! Focus, Sloane!

I twisted away and this time he let me, dropping his arm and leaning back against a wall of shelves as I took a deep breath and steadied myself. Karate prepares you for chokeholds and grips, for locks and strikes, but it definitely does not prepare you for the feeling of a hot, hard cock attached to an even hotter and harder prince, and I needed a second. Maybe two.

Finally, I could think with a mostly clear head again. "What do you want, Lennox?"

"I wanted to warn you about Rhys."

There were so many things about that statement that didn't make sense. But the only thing I could articulate was, "You needed to warn me in a *closet*?"

He frowned. "Well, obviously, we can't be

seen talking like this. Think of my reputation, darling."

"I'm not your darling," I said irritably. I wasn't darling; I was deadly, and also it was very unfair how sexy the word *darling* sounded with his accent.

"My apologies," Lennox said with a slicing grin. "What would you rather I call you? Poppet? Dove? My sweet, heartless huntress?"

"I'd rather you call me nothing," I said emphatically, even though I didn't *entirely* hate the way any of those endearments sounded on his lips.

Lennox kept smiling. "My nothing, my sweet nothing. Oh, I like the sound of that. It's quite Shakespearean."

I refused to indulge him a moment longer. "Okay, well, if that's all—"

The frown returned. "That's not all. I haven't warned you about Rhys yet."

"A warning is unnecessary," I told him. "I know exactly what kind of guy Rhys is."

Lennox took a step forward. In the small expanse of the closet, it brought him within touching distance again. I tried to ignore the thrill my body gave at that.

"I don't think you know at all," he said, and

for once, his voice wasn't dripping with scorn or crackling with hate. He sounded completely serious. "Rhys is practically sociopathic. He's a monster. If he asked you to the Huntington Gala, it's not because he wants to go on picnics and skip through the bloody park with you."

Irritation surged within me.

Finally! Here was my fighting instinct!

I stepped right up to Lennox and lifted my face defiantly to his. "He's already told me all of this."

Surprise moved across Lennox's aristocratic features. "He has?"

"Yes. He's been nothing but honest with me. *And* you know what else?"

Lennox's face was tilted down towards mine now, his soft blond hair tumbling over his forehead. "What else?"

"He can talk to me outside of closets. He's really romantic like that."

A muscle jumped in Lennox's jaw.

And then in an instant, his hands were on me again, dragging me against his body as he pressed his lips to my ear. "How would you, my cold, heartless sweetheart, know anything about romance?"

His words whispered warmth over my skin

and sent shivers skating down my spine.

I meant to push his hands away, I meant to wedge my elbows between us and drag them over the nerves in his forearms. I meant to shove my head into his, and then finish him off with a swift strike to the sternum.

I meant to do all of those things. But instead, I melted into him. I melted into the hard, arrogant heat of him, I melted into those sinful lips against my skin. And even though he whispered hatred and poison with those lips, my body responded like he was whispering the tenderest, naughtiest secrets instead.

"You wouldn't know, would you? Because you, my sweet, frigid *darling*, are the lowest order of virgin. You are locked up so tight that no one's ever been inside, and no one's ever even been close, have they? Is that because you won't let them or because nobody wants you—"

Of its own accord, my right hand reached up and cracked across his perfect cheek, slapping him as hard as I could. And for a single moment after that, neither of us moved. Me with my hand still stinging in midair, and him with his cheek and jaw growing red, his gold eyes blazing down at me like he wanted to light me on fire with his fury alone.

But he didn't light me on fire. He didn't even speak.

Instead, he slashed his lips over mine and took my mouth in a searing kiss.

A kiss that went from mere hungry lips to hot, searching tongues sliding against each other in seconds.

My slap hadn't affected his erection in the least. If anything, he was even harder than before, his thick column digging into my belly as he hauled me closer and closer with impatient hands, and then finally—with a growl I'd remember for the rest of my life—he shoved me up against the door.

"Wrap those legs around my waist," he grunted between wild, angry kisses. "I know you're strong enough."

"Fuck off," I retorted. But I did it anyway, because I needed—oh *God*—yes. I needed this. I needed my legs around his waist and my skirt up around my hips and his big erection right against my center. It felt *so good*.

"Bleeding Christ," Lennox muttered, tearing his mouth from mine to look down at where he rocked against me. "Even through your knickers, I can feel how hot you are."

My head dropped back against the door as he

moved his hips again, dragging his clothed erection against me, dry-fucking me. I'd never done this—I'd barely even kissed a boy before— and it felt so much better than anything I'd ever done on my own; it felt so good I thought I might die right there among the paper towels.

My panties were damp, and my nipples were beaded so tight in my bra that they ached. And every time Lennox moved, there was an answering surge from deep inside my center, an urgent clenching, like my body was trying to . . .

"Are you about to come for me?" Lennox breathed, dipping his head to bite at my neck. "Are you about to make me miserable? Hmm? Show me what I'm missing?"

I couldn't answer. I couldn't even think. My hands were in the thick silk of his hair and my lips burned without his on mine and I was so close . . .

"Can I touch it?" he asked, sliding a hand under my ass far enough that his fingertips could press against my cotton-covered seam. "Let me touch it, please, my darling—"

Nothing sounded better than his fingers on my bare skin, *nothing*, and the minute I moaned out a *yes*, his clever fingers were pushing my panties aside and searching me out, finding where I was wet and hot. Finding the place where I opened and then lingering there, pushing at my center but not quite going inside.

It was torment not having his fingers inside me, it was pure misery, and I squirmed in his arms, trying to seek out more of him.

He gave a low chuckle against my lips. "Want something, do we?"

"Screw you," I said, still squirming. Fuck, I was so close, so very close, and I knew if he touched the inside of me, if he filled me with his fingers . . .

"Then perhaps I shall remove my hand, if it doesn't matter to you either way—"

I scratched at his shoulders and back, I writhed like a wild thing, I leaned forward and bit his collarbone through his uniform shirt. "Lennox . . ."

He pulled back to look at me, his lips swollen, his hair a mess, his pupils blown so wide the gold was almost all black.

"You—" he said, but then he stopped. As if he didn't know what he wanted to say next . . .or knew but didn't want me to hear it.

It didn't matter. He could have scalded my ears with insults, he could have mocked me, debased me, recounted every horrible thing he'd ever done to me, and my body still wouldn't have cared. It was under his spell completely and utterly, it was drugged by his warm lips and rough, impatient hands, and it was poised to dissolve. And then finally, *finally*, I felt the breach of his finger.

We both froze, staring at each other.

Lennox Lincoln-Ward, prince and bully, was fingering me. And it felt better than anything in the entire world.

"This is mine," he murmured.

My eyes fluttered as he went deeper, as he resumed grinding against me with that arrogant cock. "But you hate me," I managed to whisper.

I could hear the dark promise in his voice when he said, "That's exactly why it's mine."

And I came.

To the sound of his possessive, cruel words, I came—so hard that I had to bite his blazer to keep from screaming.

Shudders moved through me, detonating around his long finger and behind my clit, and I was feral in his arms, trying to fuck his finger, trying to rub my clit against his erection, trying to hold on for dear life as my inner thighs and lower belly were seized by delicious, animal bliss.

It took so long for the climax to finish that I was gasping for breath after, that I was nearly weak with holding myself against him. I slumped back against the door, my pussy still sporadically jolting with pleasure, and looked at Lennox.

He had a wild look in his eyes—a look so unlike his usual calculated cruelty that I was almost scared.

"Don't go to the gala with Rhys," he said in a voice just as wild as his expression.

His finger was still inside me, and it was so hard not to start fucking his hand again. "Why not?" I asked. I barely recognized my own voice. It was as far from disciplined and reserved as could be—I sounded sexed-up and lazy and . . . happy?

He slid another finger inside me, and I moaned, rolling my hips. "Because this is mine now."

"I don't think so." Rich words coming from the girl currently fucking herself on his fingers.

"You made a mistake, my darling, letting me feel it, because I'm not about to let it—or you— go. And I'm certainly not going to let Rhys anywhere near this."

"You have literally zero say in who gets near me," I countered, but again, my words were lazy and husky with pleasure. Not exactly ringing with authority. "Plus I kind of want to go to the gala now."

"Then go with me."

I stopped moving and stared at him. He stared back, that wildness still in his eyes, his body taut as a wire against me.

"You've got to be joking," I said.

"I'm not."

"You hate me."

"Yes."

"You don't even want to be seen talking in public with me."

"Correct," he said.

"But now you want to go to the gala with me as your date?"

He blinked slowly, his long eyelashes framing those impossible eyes. I had the sense that even he didn't know why he wanted to go to the gala with me, but for a moment—for a stupid, dumb, terrible moment—I thought . . .

No. I wasn't foolish enough to think that he liked me. I wasn't deranged enough to think that he suffered from the same sickness I had when it came to him. But I at least thought he'd tell me that he wanted to get under my skirt again, that he wanted to kiss me again.

Instead, what he said was: "Rhys doesn't get to touch you."

Somehow *this* was what shook me down to reality.

Not the best orgasm of my life surrounded by paper towels and toilet paper.

Not him admitting—twice—that he hated me.

Not even him asking me to the gala.

But this.

This reminder that no matter how much he enjoyed mauling me in the supply closet, no matter how desperate he'd been to touch me, I was nothing more than prey to him. Prey that he'd already marked as his own and wouldn't deign to share with Rhys.

And I, Sloane Lauder—daughter without a mother, daughter of a father who chased criminals all around the world, a black belt and a badass—was not prey. Not even for beautiful boys with fingers like magic and lips like sin.

I moved out of his arms, which made his fingers slide free. My core clenched at the emptiness, but I ignored it. "I'm going with him."

He frowned down at his hand, as if unhappy that it was no longer up my skirt. Then he looked back to me. "You're going with me, Sloane. That's the end of it."

I laughed a little, astounded at his conceit.

"Do I look insane to you? I'm not picking you over him. At least he's the devil I know."

"That's because he *is* the devil," Lennox replied. "I am only a monster."

I pushed him back enough so that I could smooth my clothes and then turn to open the door. He slammed a hand up to stop me, pressing against me to whisper in my ear.

"You can't hide from me, Sloane. You've belonged to me since the day I saw you."

The first two fingers of his hand were still glistening with me, and the reminder of how they felt inside my panties was enough to make my knees weak. I somehow managed to say, "Belonged to you for *what*, Prince Lennox?"

"To toy with," he said against my ear. And then he ran his nose along the curve of my neck. "To break."

I reached back behind me and wrapped my fingers around his unsatisfied length.

He shuddered.

I squeezed.

And then his hand fell from the door as he reached for me again.

"I don't break so easy." I warned him with a final squeeze hard enough to make him growl. And then I opened the door and left him there with the paper towels.

Chapter Four

Sloane

IT WAS OFFICIAL. I was living in the twilight zone. Not only had Rhys Huntington kissed me twice now—in full view of everyone—but Lennox had just destroyed me in a supply closet with nothing more than his filthy mouth and his long fingers. For the first time in my entire life, I had a boy striving for my attention.

Two boys, in fact.

And how do you actually feel about that?

Oh, Rhys was attractive. I wasn't blind. He was *very* pretty to look at. But there was something cold and distant about him. Something told me ice wouldn't melt in his mouth. But he was a very good kisser.

Although, I wondered just how irritated Serafina was about the whole thing.

She hated Rhys. No doubt. But I was an expert at watching people. And there was something about her that was fascinated by him. It could well have been that she wanted to dissect him like a frog, but it couldn't be denied that there was a part of her that perked to attention every time he was nearby. Or, maybe she just liked fighting with him.

Then why were you *kissing him?*

That was a good question. Maybe because for once, it was nice to feel pretty. Desirable. Ninety-nine point nine percent of the time, I'd tamped down any and all of my femininity. I wasn't a beauty queen like Sera, or hell, even Iris. I was pretty, but I didn't have that knockout body. I was built lean and athletic. Twiggy, actually. And I learned early on that it's better to have personality and skills than it was to have beauty.

Or at least, that's what you've told yourself.

Whatever. The point was, Rhys Huntington had taken to kissing me. And I still wasn't entirely sure how I felt about it.

I liked being kissed. Kisses, for all intents and purposes, were *awesome.* And every time he kissed me, something warm blossomed in my chest. It was pleasant. And he was a very, very good kisser. I just—I don't know.

Rhys kissing me was nothing like what hap-

pened with Lennox in the supply closet. At. All.
That was wild, and fiery. And hot. Like I was
being burned alive from the inside out.

The way Iris talked about her and Keaton
made it seem like there were firecrackers all
around her, but also this sense of tenderness.
Lennox certainly hadn't been tender. God, Iris
would know what to do. I missed her terribly. But
she was in Paris, having left school early to go live
her best arty life. Keaton went to see her every
other weekend. That's what happened when your
family had a private jet.

The fact that she'd gone off to Paris, leaving
us mere mortals behind, made me wish it was
summer and we could go and visit her already.
But we'd gotten good with the online video chats.
I checked my watch. Sera, Aurora, and I would
wait up until one or two in the morning to talk to
her.

She and Keaton were doing the long-distance
thing, and then he was going to see her for the
holidays. Then it would again be back to long
distance until the summer. God, they were so in
love. It was crazy. But Rhys and I, we *weren't* that.
And maybe I was just fascinated by him. Or
fascinated by the fact he'd taken notice of me.
Because the question was, why had he taken

notice of me? Why now?

I'd known Rhys since freshman year. He wasn't exactly nice. He could be excessively cruel. Not usually to me though. It was usually the people who dicked with him. If you dicked with him, god help you. He was savage. Unrelenting. And he'd make your life a living hell. I'd mostly just kept out of his way because I already had Lennox obsessed with breaking me—I didn't need anything worse than perverted bathroom graffiti from Rhys.

The sudden interest . . . there was something behind it, and I couldn't quite figure it out.

Maybe he was just bored.

Then why did you let him kiss you?

Maybe I was bored too.

Or you can't have who you really want?

I swallowed that down. Lennox's kisses were . . . different. I could still feel the tingle of his lips sliding over mine. The way he'd gripped the back of my neck, holding me in place as he completely devoured my mouth. Lennox's kisses were dangerous. Designed to fog the brain and then make it impossible to think. I had a sharp mind. I liked my mind. And PS, why was Lennox even kissing me? He was very clear on his hatred of me.

And I hated him.

Liar.

Okay fine. Maybe I didn't hate him exactly, but god, I loathed the way he treated me. He was cruel in the way only the powerful can be in that off-hand manner, giving out insults in mini barbs. I could hold my own. The things he said to me didn't hurt. But that kiss, at the supply closet today, *that* one hurt. I knew he was only kissing me, touching me, because Rhys had. I didn't want to be some dick measuring competition for them. I just wanted someone to notice me. Why was that super hard?

My cellphone rang as I made it to my room. I was alone, so I plopped on the bed and tossed my bag as I fished the phone out of my back pocket. "Hey, Dad."

"Sloane, how was class today?"

"How do you know I went to class and I wasn't out ditching?"

"You're my daughter. You don't ditch. You like rules."

"That I do. It's alarming you know me so well. Shouldn't you factor in at any point that I am a teenager?"

"You are a teenager, but you are cut from the same cloth as I am. You like rules. You like following them. If you ditch, there would be a damn good reason."

I hated that he was right. Maybe a part of me wanted to ditch. Cut class. It was a rite of passage. Why hadn't I done it more?

I shoved that thought aside. "What's up, Dad?"

"What, I can't just call my daughter?"

"It's not Sunday. You always call on Sundays, 10 a.m."

He sighed. "You know, I do miss you at other times other than Sundays at ten."

I winced. I hadn't meant to hurt him. "I'm sorry. It's just unusual, I guess. Is everything okay?"

There was a beat of silence. "Yes, everything is fine. I'm healthy, before you start worrying about that."

My mother had died of cancer when I was eight. And with Dad's job, he couldn't drag me around all the time, so he'd sent me to boarding school. But he'd taken to reassuring me of his health all the time. Probably so I didn't worry. Unfortunately, that just made me worry more. "You're sure you're okay?"

"Definitely okay—a little tired, maybe, since this Constantine case has blown up. I suppose

Cash hasn't been doing anything suspicious lately?"

"Like what? Trying to fence stolen Bronze Age burial goods in rural Vermont?"

"Ha," Dad said dryly. "Very funny, and you know what I mean. The Constantines act like they're above anything criminal, but we all know that's hardly the case. They're just better at hiding it is all, and I've got authorities from three different bureaus breathing down my neck about what they've imported in the last year alone."

Cash's mother apparently had a yen for collecting antiques—the kind of antiques that were illegally extracted from war zones or unethically lifted from dig sites before they could be catalogued—that sort of thing. Dad had asked more than once if I'd ever seen Cash doing anything untoward, but Cash was a floppy-haired sophomore who liked boobs and extra tacos on taco Tuesday, so obviously not. He was as clean as a whistle. A whistle who loved cafeteria food and boobs.

"Hey, I wanted to ask," Dad continued, "you're close to that Lincoln-Ward kid, right?"

I frowned. "Lennox? We're not friends, but I know him, I guess."

"Right, right. Listen, can you do me a favor

and keep an eye on him?"

"An eye? For you?" I was honestly baffled. Lennox wasn't a *good* person, but it wasn't like he was collecting stolen antiques like Cash's mom. "Why?"

My dad cleared his throat. "You remember his father? The investigation that put him in prison?"

Uneasiness dripped down my neck like cold water. "Yes. You said you consulted on it once."

Another throat clearing. "I wasn't—well, I wasn't *entirely* forthright about that. I did work on the case quite a bit, in fact. I was the arresting agent on the scene."

I took a moment to respond, because I wasn't sure *how* to respond. Dad and I never lied to each other. Not ever. Lying was what art thieves and con men and fences did—not family. "Why didn't you tell me?"

It could explain why Lennox disliked me so much . . . although that didn't really make sense either. Not if he'd told Aurora that he *wanted* his dad in prison. Why hate the daughter of the man who put him there then?

"It's not a stage of my career I'm proud of," Dad said slowly. "It's a little difficult to look back at the things I did then, much less talk about them."

"Things you did during the investigation?" I asked, the uneasiness growing into horror. "Like unethical things?"

"Oh god, no, no, not that," Dad said. "Nothing illegal or immoral. I just didn't handle the . . . political . . . aspects of the case very well."

"Political? Like intra-bureau politics?"

"Among other things," Dad murmured. "But nevertheless, the older Lincoln-Ward keeps coming back to haunt me, like a bad penny. A bad, *conniving* penny. He's making noise about an appeal now, of all things, and we're still trying to figure out where he's hid the rest of his money to get the victims the restitution they deserve. And it's possible that he squirrelled that money away for his kids somehow. Which maybe they're aware of, maybe they aren't. Which is why if you could keep an eye on him . . . see if he's doing anything other than the norm . . ."

He trailed off. I was staring at my ceiling, seeing nothing, my chest tight.

"You want me to . . . what? Tail him?"

"Of course not, honey," Dad said, his tone the epitome of reason and sanity, as if *I* were the unreasonable one right now. "You know, it merely would be great if you can get information from his laptop. Or something."

I frowned, the unease making my stomach cramp. Illegality shouldn't bother me; I knew that on an abstract, intellectual level. Sometimes there was a greater need and all. But it was like the lying . . . I didn't think we were supposed to do that. I didn't think we *did* do that.

"At school, he must leave it around sometimes," Dad prompted.

I frowned even deeper at that. On the one hand, my father, my idol, basically, was asking me to take part in a job to actually assist him at work. He knew how much I wanted to be like him. How much I wanted to work in intelligence one day. So this was the opportunity of a lifetime. On the other hand, it made me feel squicky.

Oh, Lennox was cruel. And worse, he was deliberate in his cruelness. He'd tortured me for years. But there was something about *this* that made me feel like I shouldn't.

"Sloane," my father prompted. "Can you do it?"

I'd been silent for too long. "Yeah, but Dad. I mean, Lennox is just a kid. He's eighteen like me, so there's a great possibility that he's not involved with his father. We're too young for that."

"Like you're too young to be creeping around campus solving certain problems for your peers?"

"Uh . . ."

Dad laughed a little. "Yes, I know about that. And no, you're not in trouble. I know you do what you do in order to help the people you know need it. Which is why I'm asking this of you—I know you're capable and lots of people need your help right now. Not just me, but all the victims Lincoln-Ward swindled. If he succeeds in moving the last of his money around, we may never be able to return it to the people it was stolen from."

I sighed. He was right.

Truth was, I didn't *know* Lennox that well. I mean, I did, but it was more on an emotional visceral level. Something like *this*, I couldn't say whether he would or wouldn't do it. I had no idea.

"Listen, Sloane, I know you've been wanting to intern at INTERPOL before you go to Georgetown. I think we can work that out. This is a small opportunity for you to prove yourself."

Way to twist the knife, Dad. "Fine. I'll do it. Just information from his laptop, right?"

"Yeah, that's it. Nothing else. Obviously, I don't want you to take any unnecessary risks."

"I won't," I mumble, a knot forming in my gut.

"We want information only. Strictly for sur-

60

veillance. Do not get any more involved than that. You can do that, right?"

I swallowed. "It'll be easy, Dad. He leaves his laptop everywhere." Actually, I didn't know if that was true. I'd seen him and the Hellfire boys sitting around it watching dumb videos on the lawn a few times, but that was only when the weather was nice, which November in Vermont rarely was. But sometimes in the classroom he left it lying around, so I just had to find my window. Enough to do a recon. "I can get it done. When do you need it by?"

"Within the next week or two."

"Consider it done."

He was silent for a beat. "I knew I could count on you."

As he hung up, the words *I love you* were at the tip of my tongue. But I knew they'd only be met with a *me too*. So I hung up as well.

Just how the hell are you going to get this done?

I could do it. I could do anything. Even if it meant getting a little closer to Lennox Lincoln-Ward than I wanted to.

Chapter Five

Lennox

I DON'T BREAK so easily . . .

Sloane's words echoed through my mind as anger and lust hit me in the gut. It had been three days since the cupboard, three days since I'd dry-shagged her with her uniform skirt pushed up around her hips. Three days since I informed her that she was going to the gala with me, damn it all.

Because she was *mine*. And she had been since I was fourteen, she just hadn't known it yet.

Mine to torture. Mine to break.

I *deserved* her.

"Daddy wants a call," an airy voice said from behind me in my room.

I turned from my desk to see my sister throwing herself into my chair, as if she belonged here and not in her own bloody dorm. As if my bloody door hadn't been locked.

I scowled. "How did you get in here?"

Aurora kicked her feet in the air before grinning at me. Normally her hair was as unnaturally blonde as mine, but for some unknowable sister reason, she'd dyed it black last summer. Now whenever she smiled with her gold eyes and midnight hair, she looked like she was about to carve out a boy's heart. With a dull knife. While it was still beating in his chest.

"Sloane's been teaching me a few tricks."

My body gave an automatic stir at the mention of her name. "Of course. Probably learned it from her father."

Aurora leaned her head back and closed her eyes. "You have to stop blaming her for what her father did. I have."

"Her father *ruined* us. Ruined our mother. Ruined everything."

My sister made a face, her eyes still closed. "No, Len, *our* father ruined everything. Remember?"

I didn't answer her. I didn't need to, because I did remember.

As children, we only knew our British billionaire father worked in the city doing something with money. *Like a banker, but an artist too*, he'd told us once. *I paint entire worlds with money. I paint a new life for people.*

Of course he was an artist; that made sense to us. He was creative and playful and charming— the kind of father who would come home late from a trip and wake us up to eat all the treats he'd brought for us. The kind of father who'd play hide and seek, who'd make silly faces at the table, who'd give us ice lollies whenever we scraped our knees.

We worshipped him; even our mother worshipped him. He was often late, often absent when he shouldn't have been, often caught in small lies that had seemed harmless at the time. But he was so charming, so funny and so full of smiles, it was impossible to stay angry with him, and our mother never could.

Until the day it all came crashing down.

Aurora and I were thirteen—me at school in England, her at a Swiss boarding school—when it happened: a years-long international investigation came to an end, definitively proving my father was the mastermind behind a sprawling Ponzi scheme that totaled billions and billions. Proving my father was a swindler and a liar who had defrauded thousands of investors.

A *painter of money* indeed.

If that had been the worst of it, we would have already been devastated. Gutted and humiliated. But the day they came to arrest my father, he wasn't at home, he wasn't at his city office—he was in a hotel in Monte Carlo.

With a woman who was *not* our mother. A woman he'd apparently been with many, many times before.

The paps caught it all. Their embraces on the balcony before, their flushed faces as they were both led out of the hotel in handcuffs after.

And so our family shame was complete. Our father was not only a deceiver but a cheater; he'd thrown money onto the flames of his greed and thrown the dignity of a princess back in her face. The tabs loved it—the con artistry and the philandering—and so did the more serious news outlets, and within days, both Aurora and I were pulled from our schools for our own safety. Our father had defrauded too many people—too many wealthy people—and we were the targets they could reach, the scapegoats for our father's sins. Even with the security the Liechtensteiner government gave us being the grandchildren of the Queen, we were still in danger.

Of course all joint accounts of my parents were seized—our home in England too. Luckily mother had her own royal trust accounts and we had our untouchable trust funds which we were able to access when we'd turned eighteen. But we'd had to move back to Liechtenstein; we'd had to find new and more secure schools to attend.

We were lucky—I knew that. How many families have princesses for mothers? Queens for grandmothers? The retreat of the Lincoln-Wards was a retreat into shame and humiliation, yes, but it wasn't a retreat into abject poverty. Aside from the pride and the hole our father had ripped through the world, we would survive. Comfortably, if not happily.

But I could never forget that *everything* we lost—and how publicly we lost it—could be laid at the feet of one man alone.

Nathan Lauder.

Former FBI agent. Head of the National Central Bureau for INTERPOL in the States. It was Nathan who'd taken the first fraud claims against my father, and it was Nathan who'd spearheaded the entire investigation.

For that, I would have forgiven him. His job was to stop criminals, and my father was a criminal, after all. A criminal who I knew roundly deserved every day in prison he got. No, it wasn't the arrest or the conviction that infuriated me, that made me crave revenge.

It was that Nathan *chose* not to bring my father in quietly, privately. Nathan *chose* someplace tawdry and public.

He'd not only ruined us, but he'd made it a spectacle, made it so garishly and vulgarly visible.

And I'd hated him for it.

After the arrest, I had a lot of time in a new home, in a different country, to think about how much I hated Nathan Lauder. I had a lot of time to research him—to cajole, beg, and command my grandmother's security people to research him too.

Which was when I first heard the name Sloane.

Sloane Lauder. His daughter, my age.

There were no pictures of her online—Nathan was too careful for that—no other information at all actually, save for her name listed in a single obituary. Her mother—his wife—had died when she was young. No siblings, no extended family. They lived in D.C.

I used to fantasize about growing up and finding her. I'd humiliate her the way Nathan had humiliated *us* and see how much he liked it then. Having his precious daughter dragged through the tabloid mud, having all of his family's dirty linens flapping in the very, very public breeze.

But of course that hadn't been necessary, had it? Because I'd come to Pembroke, and whom should I find?

Sloane herself. *Here.*

Now.

Gracefully lethal. Green-eyed and quiet.

She held herself with a discipline that fascinated and enraged me—actually everything about her fascinated and enraged me.

And nothing enraged me more than her soft, lush mouth.

She had a pout that was made for kissing, licking, and sex—not for getting up at 6 a.m. and running five miles, only to turn around and train for hours in the gym the moment classes ended. Not for the careful, expressionlessness she always kept on her face, like she was already training to be a spy. Not for the way she never gave anything away, ever, even when I pushed and pushed and pushed . . .

Except for the cupboard.

Fuck me, the cupboard. I'd finally felt that plush mouth for myself, felt it warm and drugging against my lips. And her soft, tight cunt . . .

"Len," Aurora said impatiently, "are you going to call Daddy with me or not?"

I leaned back in my chair, thinking about it for exactly one second. "No."

"You're so eager to hate Sloane, yet you hate Daddy too. Don't you remember anything from Mass? We're supposed to forgive people."

"Like how you're forgiving Phineas, for example?"

She shot upright, glaring at me. "Low blow, Lennox, even for you."

I held up my hands. "I don't even know what he *did* last summer, Sister Dearest. Only that he seems to be coping with it by shagging half the school, and you're coping with it by making his life a living hell. *And* I don't actually give a shit, I'm just pointing out that it's rather hypocritical of you to want me to forgive people when you're constantly planning Phineas's untimely death."

"Fine," she bit out, standing up and striding to the door. "I'll call Daddy alone then."

"Tatty byes, Aurora."

She turned the handle and then paused. "You know he wants to help make things right, Len. He's trying to be better."

I let out a long breath.

I was a bastard, yes, and a bully definitely, but I did love my sister. It gave me no pleasure to say the words I said next. Not to the girl who'd once chased Daddy through the gardens right alongside me, who'd eaten sweets on his knee next to me while he told us all about Germany or Italy or Japan or wherever else he'd been.

"He's lying, Aurora," I said, studying her face. "You know that, right? He's trying to charm you. Swindle you back into loving him."

She smiled sadly, as if she knew that just as well as I did.

"Better than trying to swindle us out of our trust funds at least," she said, and then she cracked open the door and left.

The trust funds. The two protected assets the government didn't seize, because our father had made our grandparents the trustees, and therefore he couldn't touch them. He'd been clever enough to do that at least, although he hadn't been clever enough not to get caught.

But because he couldn't touch them, because they'd been preserved, I had no doubt he had his eye on them. Especially if he won his latest round of appeals and had his sentence reduced. Wouldn't he love to be released and immediately have access to millions of pounds sterling?

I don't think so.

I turned back to my laptop and clicked open the email I'd been about to read before Aurora barged in. It was from the lawyer who managed our trust funds—a lawyer I could trust. A lawyer who was conveniently—at least for me—intimidated by my mother's family and the crown which came with it.

I scanned the email before opening up a fresh word processor file, writing a letter I'd been drafting in my head for over a year. I rubbed at my chest as I wrote it, feeling something strange. It certainly wasn't happiness, but maybe it was something close.

Satisfaction. Gratification, maybe.

Well, why wouldn't I be gratified? Together, the lawyer and I had devised a very clever path through the warren of trust stipulations. We had figured out a way to move substantial chunks of money through various systems until it was allocated where I saw fit.

Investments into my own future, as it were.

Never let it be said that a prince would be a pauper, I thought as I closed out the email and then shut the laptop. *Father, you taught me better than you can ever know.*

Chapter Six

Sloane

Lennox, it turned out, was a lot less freewheeling with his laptop than I thought he'd be. Or perhaps he was just more interested in me since I'd shamelessly come all over his fingers a few days before. Because now there was no leaving his things unattended in the library, there was no milling around the classroom during free time and leaving his laptop at his desk. Now he was right next to me, always sticking close, always sliding in with little verbal jabs and slices, cutting me into pieces with his cold smiles. Wherever I was, Lennox somehow found a reason to be also, and so there was no way to do what Dad had asked and search out what he wanted.

And then Thursday morning came, and just like every other morning, Lennox was on the outdoor track with me, following me through the early morning fog as I started my laps. I could hear his footfalls behind me—soft and graceful, like a cat's—I could hear his breathing, steady and even. No huffing and puffing for this prince, no way. He was all cool and arrogant control all the time. When he played, when he worked out. Even when he tormented me.

I'd only ever seen him lose control when he—

My cheeks flushed as I remembered the closet. He'd been wild to kiss me. Wild to touch me between my legs.

Wild to *keep* me.

At that thought, I sped up—not sure if I was running faster because I was angry or creeped out or turned on . . . or some fucked up combination of all three.

Predictably, he sped up behind me, as if reluctant to let any more space between us.

Rhys doesn't get to touch you.

You've belonged to me since the day I saw you.

To toy with. To break.

Fuck it, I *was* angry. He'd treated me like trash since day one, and now when another boy was taking notice of me for the first time ever, he suddenly had a problem?

He got to be first in line to treat me like trash, was that it?

It had been infuriating before, when it only affected me. But now his abrupt possessiveness was keeping me from helping my father, which by extension was keeping me from my dream of following in my father's footsteps. It had to stop.

I wouldn't be his plaything. I *couldn't.* There was too much at stake.

Anger flooded me, and determination too, and I spun around to face him, my hands coming up automatically in a guard position, as if I were about to spar.

Lennox's reflexes were irritatingly sharp, because he was already stopped by the time I'd turned, his mouth in a flat line and one eyebrow raised. Only the quick thrum of his pulse above the collar of his too-expensive workout shirt betrayed that he'd been exerting himself. "My god, Lauder, are we about to start a fracas right here on the track? Am I going to regret forcing my poor security fellow to stay at the track entrance?"

I lowered my fists, finally realizing they were raised. Too much karate or too much time with Dad, I guess, because I knew Lennox wouldn't try to hurt me, not like this. Punches and strikes weren't his way. He preferred to hurt me more . . . *creatively.*

"What do you want?" I asked him, tense and

coiled all over with fury and frustration. "Why do you come out here every morning? Why won't you leave me alone?"

Fog drifted around him as he took a step closer. "You already know what I want."

"No! I don't! And you know what? I don't think you know what you want either!"

His golden eyes flashed. "I know exactly what I want. For you to stay away from Rhys."

"It's none of your business, Prince Lennox. Just like my morning run is none of your business."

His expression sharpened and so did his voice. "Haven't you figured it out yet, my sweet nothing? You belong to me, and I'm not in the habit of letting my things go unattended. Especially when they are so . . ." His eyes dropped to where my fists were still balled at my sides. ". . . willful."

"The closet changes nothing," I said.

"About that and nothing else, you are right, darling." He stepped closer again, and this time, we were close enough to touch. Close enough that I had to tilt my head back to look into his sharp, sculpted face, close enough that I could see how the gold and amber spun together in his eerie eyes. "The closet didn't change anything, because you were already mine. Before I tasted you. Before I felt your cunt against my hand. You were mine before all of that."

Jesus, he wasn't a prince, he was a pirate. He'd spotted me on the horizon and decided to wreck me before I'd ever even known his name.

"Get some therapy, your highness. I'm not *anyone's.*"

Another flash of those eyes and he reached for me, like he was going to pull me close, and I dodged him easily. He reached again, this time half lunging at me, and he was quick, so fucking quick, that he nearly had his arms around me.

But I don't spend every free second training for nothing. I let him get close—let his arms start to circle me—and then with a hook of my foot around the back of his and with my shoulder pushed into his chest, I had him flat on his back. I went down with him, and by the time he'd stopped falling, I was straddling his hips with my forearm to his throat. We'd gone down in the practice field in the middle of the track, and I could feel the cool, wet grass through my knees.

The fog around us was thick enough that we couldn't be seen, but I still checked around us with quick flicks of my eyes. I trusted that Lennox really had made his security guy stay off the track, but still. The last thing I needed was an angry Liechtensteiner guard shouting at me in German and turning this into an international incident.

Convinced we were alone and out of sight—*thank you, fog*—I turned my attention back to the beautiful, heartless boy underneath me.

"Leave. Me. Alone," I said between clenched teeth.

"No," he replied, as coolly as if he were sitting bored on a throne somewhere. "I won't."

I pressed harder with my forearm. Not enough to choke him, but enough so that he knew that I could if I wanted to. "I mean it, Lennox. No more following me. No more shitty remarks. No more lube in my bag or caring about who I kiss. Keep my name out of your mouth and my face out of your thoughts. Got it?"

Lennox almost seemed amused. "I've gotten to you rather terribly, haven't I?" Satisfaction curled through his voice.

I leaned forward. "No. You haven't."

But leaning forward was a mistake, because now I could see, in utter and perfect detail, the tempting lines of his mouth. The sharply masculine peaks of his upper lip, the firm but plush bow of the lower. And below me, where I straddled his hips, I could feel the effect this position was having on him. The silky material of his athletic shorts hid nothing of his desire, and my running pants were no better. They'd be damp soon, if they weren't already.

Unconsciously, without meaning to, I rocked forward over him, rubbing my sex against his erection like a needy kitten. The corner of his mouth sharpened—an almost smirk—even as his hips lifted to give me more.

"See?" he said.

"You're not—I don't—you haven't gotten to me." But the lie was in my body, in how I tried to fuck him through our clothes, even as my forearm kept him pinned to the ground underneath me. The lie was in my voice, which was breathy and husky and transparently aroused.

"Oh, but I have," he said, his mouth still in that bitter smile. I felt his hands curl over my hips—something that would have been a threat if we'd been truly fighting, but of course, this wasn't a fight, not really. I . . . I didn't know what this was, exactly, but I did know that whatever it was meant he could touch my hips like he was now.

And slide his hand across the flat plane of my stomach and find the hem of my tank top.

And tug down the waistband of my pants and push his fingers into my panties and between my legs.

My eyes fluttered closed as he found me, stroked me. There was no hiding that he *got to me* now, there was no hiding how much my body reacted to his presence. I was wet enough to be slippery, wet enough that even he seemed surprised—although that surprise faded quickly into a dark satisfaction.

"Good," he whispered. "I refuse to be the only one."

I kept my forearm on his throat as he slid up to my clit. He knew *just* how to touch, *just* how to rub. Fast then slow. Circles then up and down. I hated thinking about all the practice he'd had, I hated knowing scores and scores of girls had come before me . . . but I didn't hate it so much I'd make him stop. Not at all.

I was a simple girl, after all. A direct girl. A good spy would use any means at her disposal to meet her goal, after all, and if my goal was to have a toe-curling orgasm on the practice field inside the school track while straddling the school's resident bully . . .

Except that a good spy would also not be fooling around with her mark.

Outside.

When his security detail could be anywhere.

"When you come, my sweet nothing, consider this: if you aren't mine, then why is it that I find this pretty pussy wet for me every time I touch it?"

"Shut up," I told him, riding his touch, feeling everything between my knees and my navel grow taut and trembling. "You're ruining it."

"Oh," he said softly, smiling again. "I don't think I am. And if you come for me like this, just imagine all the other ways I could do it . . ."

I didn't have to imagine much. His mouth, cruel and soft all at once, the kind of mouth that promised vicious and punishing pleasure. And that thick erection was underneath me again, huge and hard . . .

My orgasm came at me like a freight train, running me over, laying me flat. I cried out and bucked against Lennox's hand, coming and coming and unable to stop, unable to think, unable to do anything but *feel*. That powerful but elegant hand in my panties, the firm bulge of him beneath me. The cold grass wet against my knees and the fog clinging to my throat and chest as I arched against the feeling.

And then it faded—the tight waves in my sex and my belly slowly growing looser, more languid—until I was just a girl slumped over a boy in the grass, with his hand in her pants and her forearm on his throat.

No.

Not just a girl, not just a boy.

I was Sloane Lauder, and this was Lennox Lincoln-Ward.

What the *fuck* was wrong with me?

Without a word, I scrambled off Lennox, retreating back several steps as panic clawed at my throat. People thought I felt nothing, that I was a robot or some kind of stoic, but nothing could have been further from the truth. I felt *everything*, every single thing, which was why I needed my father's lessons and karate so much. I'd needed to learn control, to learn patience and discipline, and it was only the years of training, years of practicing calm, cool control, that helped me find my breath again.

I looked down at Lennox, who was now up on his elbows in the grass staring at me like there was going to be a test later. The fact that I was leaving him high and dry for the second time this week didn't escape me. How could it, when the evidence was so proudly—and urgently—tenting the front of his shorts?

"Come back here, Sloane," he said, his accent curling around the words like the fog curled around my ankles. "Come back here and finish what you started."

"No," I said. But it came out shaky and uncertain. He stared at me a moment, his chest moving up and down, his pulse pounding in his throat.

"Suit yourself," he said, as if he didn't care at all, and then he slid his fingers in his mouth—the same fingers that had been in my panties just moments earlier—sucking them, licking them, getting them wet. And without a single beat of hesitation, he pushed his hand past the waistband of his shorts and took a hold of himself, giving his length a short, rough stroke with his wet hand.

A sound left me then, a *guh* noise, like I'd just been punched in the stomach during sparring practice. Even though his dick and his fist were covered by the material of his shorts, seeing him lick his hand—the hand that tasted like *me*—and then stroke himself was painfully hot. A conflagration of crude and arrogant sexiness that should have been straight up illegal.

A jolt of fresh need sparked between my thighs, and I almost wanted to join him, to kneel beside him and wrap my hand over his hand and help him.

A bell tolled through the fog, as familiar as it

was solemn. Seven a.m. Classes would start in 90 minutes. More importantly, various teams would be out for their morning practices momentarily, and we'd no longer be alone on the field.

To my great disappointment (and shame at the aforementioned disappointment), Lennox realized this too and stopped that wonderful stroking motion.

He pulled his hand free and rolled to his feet with enviable grace, although there was nothing graceful about the prominent column of his cock still pushing against the front of his shorts. "We're not done," he promised. "Saturday. The gala. We're finishing this."

"I told you," I said, shaking my head, as if I could shake off the strange slick of regret spilling through my chest. "I'm going with Rhys."

"Maybe. But you won't be leaving with him," he said enigmatically, and then turned towards campus and stalked off into the fog. Within a handful of steps, he was no longer visible, and I was left alone, damp from the grass and trembling at my lack of control.

CHAPTER SEVEN

SLOANE

T HIS COULDN'T GO on.

This . . . this *hold* that Lennox had on me, it had to stop. How had I let an argument turn into a closet fingerbang? How had I let defending myself turn into a *second* fingerbang?

On the *practice field* no less?

No, I was better than this. I was better than having pants-feelings for my gold-eyed tormentor. I was better than letting my father down because I couldn't *keep control*.

"You seem, uh, intense today," Cash remarked from the bag next to mine.

I grunted in acknowledgement, giving the bag several jab-knee combinations.

"Well, more intense than usual," Cash amended. "You okay? Are you having trouble with one of your . . . you know . . . *cases?*"

He whispered the last part as if my helping people around the school was some kind of state secret. It was kind of cute, actually.

I delivered two more combos—hard and quick enough to send the bag swinging—and then turned to face the sophomore. Like his cousin, Keaton, Cash was blond and tall and broad-shouldered, although unlike Keaton, he hadn't yet filled in all that height with muscle yet. He would though; he had the kind of frame that promised power and strength. But I knew he felt self-conscious about his still-wiry body. Enough that he joined me in the gym every chance he got.

At least, that was *one* of the reasons he joined me in the gym.

The other reason was fairly apparent in the way his eyes kept flicking down to my damp sports bra and sweat-slick stomach.

"I'm fine," I said, tilting my chin up in the universal *eyes up, buddy* move.

He flushed and locked eyes with me, swallowing with what looked like embarrassment. Poor kid. He really was a sweetheart.

"You don't seem fine," he said, and I had to admire his balls. Not many people dared to disagree with me. "Can I help?"

I shook my head automatically. I didn't accept

help for anything; it wasn't in my nature. And I could hardly explain the problem to Cash. Either of the problems, really—neither how I accidentally kept dry-humping Lennox Lincoln-Ward, nor how my father needed me to scrape up illegal dirt on Lennox.

A prickle of guilt needled through my chest as I remembered how my father was also investigating Cash's family.

Antiquities fraud was antiquities fraud—if his relatives had done it, then that was that and they deserved to be investigated. But looking at this cute puppy of a sophomore, with all that messy hair and those hopeful eyes, I just . . .

Well, I didn't feel awesome about it. That was all.

"If I can help with anything, let me know," he said softly.

I didn't love lying, but if I was going to be a good spy, I'd need to embrace it, so I forced myself to nod and say, "I will."

He smiled—a slightly crooked smile with a megawatt dimple in each cheek. He really was going to be a heartbreaker soon. "And if all else fails, go full WWJBD, am I right?" He clapped my shoulder and then left the bags, grabbing his water bottle and trotting off to the locker room to change out.

WWJBD?

What would Jason Bourne do if he had to look at Lennox's laptop?

I stared at the bag for a moment, stunned at my own ineptitude.

I'd been going about this all wrong, searching for windows of opportunity the way a civilian would. Looking for the easiest solutions, the most obvious ones.

But Jason Bourne didn't search for windows of opportunity—he *made* his own windows.

Or crashed through them dramatically, but whatever. That didn't materially change my point.

The point was Jason Bourne would find a way to Lennox's laptop no matter what. And I would too.

SEVEN HOURS LATER, and I was really, really realizing why Jason Bourne only did the shit he did in the movies and not in real life.

I was a dab hand at picking locks—a skill Aurora had taken up with ease when I taught her—but I knew going into his room through the door was a no-go, no matter how late and seemingly asleep the dorm was. Lennox had a twin arrangement to what Aurora had in the girls' dorm: his security team slept on the same floor, and one member was always awake, patrolling the building. Additionally, there were cameras watching the hallways—monitored more or less consistently by the team—and the last thing I wanted was for there to be any record of me doing anything near Lennox's room.

So the interior of the building was out. But the exterior . . .

Pembroke was an old school, and while an old school meant constant renovations and unreliable air conditioning, it also made for *very* climbable exteriors. Sills and lintels and gables and string courses and entablatures and trellises. *Trellises.* I mean, what level of trust do you have in your students if you cover the outside of their dorm with trellises? That's just asking for people to sneak out.

Or *in*, in my case.

I knew the way from my previous lube and toothpaste missions, so I had a plan. I glanced behind me to make sure the campus lawn was still completely and utterly empty, and then I made my careful way up and over to the window I wanted, using the trellis and the occasional lintel to climb it. It was cold enough that my hands already hurt, even inside my thin leather gloves. My breath puffed out in thick, white clouds every time I exhaled.

Dad would hate that I'm doing this.

He would hate it because not only was it dangerous, but because it was legally dicey.

And by legally dicey, I meant *very, very illegal.*

But part of me suspected he knew I'd have to bend some rules in order to get what he wanted, and I figured he wanted the info more than he wanted me to have a rigid code of ethics.

And it was okay that my code of ethics wasn't that rigid, right? I mean, I wouldn't call it flaccid—I had some hard limits around what I considered right and wrong—but a little laptop spelunking didn't bother me. And neither did a little window-peeping.

When I got to my destination, I raised myself high enough on the trellis that I could peer inside. And what I saw there satisfied me. I'd made a pit stop at Rhys's window on the hunch that the Hellfire Club would be in there, doing whatever it was they did when they weren't making the rest of the school miserable. They were probably deflowering virgins or drinking the tears of the damned or something equally monstrous— although when I finally got a good look inside, it appeared that they were all arranged around Rhys's TV, watching an episode of a reality show about drag queens. Keaton Constantine was arguing with Phineas Yates about who actually won the lip-synching competition, and the argument erupted in some kind of wrestling/fisticuffs scenario that had equal parts laughter and yelling. I was about to scan the room more thoroughly when Rhys—who was sprawled on his bed like a Roman emperor—slowly swiveled his head toward the window. As if he sensed my presence.

Shit.

I ducked lower on the trellis, knowing full well I hadn't made any noise, but also knowing full well that if Rhys actually came to check the window, I'd be hosed.

WWJBD?

Jason Bourne would probably fling himself into the bushes below and then sprint off to find a car chase to get involved in, honestly, but I didn't have ankles of steel. Or a car.

Instead, I trellis-scrambled—quietly—over to the corner of the building and edged around it, praying Rhys hadn't decided to come look out his window. Which, given the lack of yelling/cat-calling/devilish laughter, he hadn't. Thank god.

Only a few more bays down, and I found myself safely on Lennox's windowsill, perched like a pigeon. Well, okay. A pigeon if it had a boot collection that would put the *Matrix* franchise to shame. I paused for a moment and took stock of what I'd seen in Rhys's room. I'd seen *all* the boys there, right? Including Lennox? Surely, I had. Surely, he was in there, arguing about wigs and lip-synching with everyone else.

Which meant I was all clear to do what I needed to do next.

Like all the rooms in this building, Lennox's had a casement window, which usually meant a vertical latch, but in the case of this old window, there wasn't a proper latch at all, just a hook and eye lock painted over so many times that the hook was too fat to properly rest in the eye anyway. I pulled a slender jab saw from my boot and slid it into the frame. With an embarrassingly little amount of effort, I had the hook undone and half the window swinging open.

I was, as they say in the movies, *in*.

The room was dark and silent, just like I'd anticipated. Excellent. I lowered my feet carefully to the floor, and then once I was off the sill, I swung the window mostly closed behind me, clamping off the flow of chilly air. The last thing I wanted was for Lennox to come back to his room and find it strangely cold.

I used the moonlight to navigate over to his desk where his laptop sat on a surface cluttered with finance magazines and newspapers printed in German. I slid into the desk chair and opened it up, not surprised to see that it was password protected, but not happy about it either.

I had something for this, a little toy I'd lifted from Dad last year: a smartphone loaded with just one program. I could plug it into almost any device running standard software and bypass a one-step password lock. It wouldn't work on anything truly protected—nothing governmental or corporate—but for personal devices and school devices, it worked like a charm. Perfect for tonight.

But suddenly, I wasn't wild about using it on Lennox's things. For the very dumb and illogical reason that using it made this whole "spying on a classmate" thing feel wrong somehow, when it didn't really before. Which made zero sense at any level, because I'd already broken into the room and planned to invade Lennox's privacy, so what was a little electronic help along the way?

And anyway, this was basically nothing I hadn't done before; I'd broken into countless classmates' phones to hunt for pictures that didn't belong to them, and I'd broken into many a dorm room to hunt for stolen jewelry, tablets, and things.

The only thing that was different this time was Lennox.

Was how I felt about him.

But if I really wanted to be an INTERPOL agent one day, I couldn't afford to be squeamish about these things, right? Even if my mark had given me the world's best orgasm on a dewy practice field that morning?

WWJBD, Sloane.

With a sigh at my flexible morals, I plugged in the smartphone and ran the program, watching the screen flash and scroll, poking idly at the newspapers on Lennox's desk. I'd taken some minimal German in middle school, and *mein Deutsch war sehr schlect*, but I could make out that the newspapers focused on business and finance, just like the magazines. Not exactly light reading.

Why would a boy in high school need to know so much about finance?

Hmm.

Maybe my father was right. Maybe Lennox *was* into something shady like his dad—going into the family business as it were.

The phone flashed a final time—unlocking the laptop screen and also showing me his password too. *Non ducor, duco.*

I am not led, I lead.

I snorted.

Lennox was a prince through and through, I guess. Or just a gigantic asshole.

I navigated over to the internet browser and opened up his email account. It was all in German, and I had to rely on my shaky language skills to skim through his folders and most of the subject lines. But even with my bad German, I could see that most of the emails in his account were from a lawyer. And several words didn't exactly need a linguistic expert to parse into meaning: bank in German was *bank*, money was *geld*, funds was *fonds*.

I replaced the password-cracker phone with a tiny external hard drive, screenshotted any email that looked suspicious, and then dropped them onto the drive.

I didn't feel disappointed that the boy I've fooled around with twice might be into some suspicious shit, I definitely wasn't feeling that *at all.*

But if I had been—if there was a tiny part of me that had fallen under his cold, delicious spell—it would have sucked. It would have felt like my stomach was crawling with bugs, it would have felt like the worst kind of reminder that Lennox was a bullying, selfish douchebag.

Ugh.

I combed through the rest of his inbox, catching everything I could, hyperaware of the clock in the corner of the screen. While I fully believed that Rhys was an actual vampire who never slept, Lennox always looked well enough rested when he joined me for my balls-early runs, which meant he probably got a decent amount of sleep. Which meant he could be heading back here at any moment. And as much as parts of my anatomy buzzed and sparked at the thought of another confrontation-that-might-lead-to-fun-times, I categorically did not want him to find me. Especially now that I knew Dad was right, and Lennox was moving his money around.

I'd finally worked my way up to the last email at the top—the most recent one—which came with several official-looking attachments.

Attachments that looked a lot like bank transfer notices.

More disappointment bug-crawled in my gut, and I found myself hesitating when it came to documenting it and saving it to the external drive.

The rest of the emails were smoking guns, but this was the bullet, and if I showed this to Dad . . .

Wait, what was I thinking? This was what Dad wanted—what *I* wanted. If Lennox had moved money someplace he shouldn't have, then that wasn't on me, that was on *him*.

I squared my shoulders and made images of everything—but stopped at the last moment, catching a few words in the email itself. Words that normally didn't come with shady bank transfers. *Familie. Haus. Universität.*

Kinder.

Nicholas.

Family. House. University. Children.

Nicholas.

Who was Nicholas? Had my father mentioned a Nicholas in his call?

My fingers paused over the keyboard, and I tried to think. Was this truly something that needed more dissection? Or was I just grasping at anything that might make Lennox seem like— well, like not his father?

Fuck.

Fuck, I didn't know.

With a muttered oath, I made screenshots and moved them over, and then I quickly deleted all the images, emptied the trash, and cleared the history of everything ever.

Time for the rest of the desk.

The middle drawer and top two drawers were painfully organized—pens, pencils, paperclips. A rubber stamp embossed with his Pembroke address and a stamp with his Liechtensteiner address. They were like the drawers of an accountant and not a horny teenage boy. The bottom drawers were all meticulously alphabetized files.

They were labelled by school subject and year, but as I went through them one by one, I saw that some labels were clearly decoys. *Hon. Global Lit. – 10ᵗʰ Grade,* for example, held more financial-looking documents in German. *Philosophy of the Greek Golden Age* was a series of letters from a British solicitor. And *Hon. Biology – 11ᵗʰ Grade* had no biology homework at all, only a single letter. Written by him to someone named Nicholas.

Nicholas.

It was tucked away inside a cream envelope that was already stamped but clearly unsealed and unsent. Like Lennox had written this letter, gotten all ready to mail it, and then balked.

The letter was short, and—*sigh*—in German again, so I could only catch a few words here and there. There was one word I could read very clearly though, and it cropped up a few times in the letter. *Vater.*

Father.

And the way Lennox had signed it—*Alles Liebe*, which meant something like *all the love to you* or *I wish all good things for you.* A very informal way to end a letter, and even though this Nicholas had been mentioned in the emails from Lennox's lawyer, it made me doubt that the letter was anything sinister or criminal. It sounded . . . affectionate.

My phone hovered above the letter. I should take a picture and give it to my father along with everything else. I should trust my instinct that this was an important secret.

But—I couldn't. I couldn't make myself take the picture.

Instead, I folded the letter back into the envelope and decided to take it with me. That way I could still have it, but I could give it a closer look before I gave it to Dad. It was a very un-Bourneish thing to do, but also it didn't feel right to do anything else. I wasn't ready to throw Lennox under the bus until I knew for certain he belonged there.

That was the thing about flexible morals—

you couldn't bend them too much, or they'd break altogether, and I wasn't ready for mine to break just yet.

I quietly closed the drawer and stood up.

Which was when I heard it.

Soft. Angry. A little urgent.

"*Sloane.*"

There was no way to describe the panic pounding through me. Pure, uncut panic, like a fist to the kidney, like a knee to the solar plexus.

I froze and kept my breathing as slow and shallow as possible. Dad had a saying from his field agent days—*you're not made till you're made*—and maybe I still had a chance to escape. Although how had I not heard him come inside? I hadn't been *that* absorbed in his emails, and surely the light from the hallway would have alerted me, even if he'd moved without a sound—

There was another soft noise, an *unf,* followed by something short and murmur-y. It was definitely Lennox, but he didn't sound anything like he normally did—all sharp edges and bitterness. He didn't sound like someone who'd just walked into his dorm and found his enemy going through his things.

Slowly—as slowly as I could manage—I turned to face the rest of the room.

It was dark enough in the far corner that I didn't see him at first, I only heard him. The rustle of blankets as someone restlessly tossed underneath. The short, irregular breaths.

Fuck. I was a terrible damn spy, because Lennox had been in his room *the entire time.* In his bed, in full view of the rest of the room, and I should have checked, I should have taken the time to really look. But instead I'd relied on a split-second glimpse through Rhys's window and the silence when I'd come in from outside, and now I was screwed.

Although . . . maybe . . .

I took a step forward. A slow, quiet one. With the laptop shut, my eyes were adjusting to the lack of light, and I could begin to make out the shape of the bed and the shape of the prince on top of it.

Another step closer, and his head tossed on the pillow, turning towards me and towards the moonlight coming in through the window. His eyes were closed, his lips parted. Even from here I could see the flush dusting his cheekbones.

He was asleep.

He was asleep.

Jesus Christ. The relief that thudded through me was so powerful that my knees practically buckled.

I hadn't been made. I hadn't been caught. I could still leave right now with everything I needed and with him none the wiser.

But I didn't leave, which was more proof that I was a terrible damn spy. I was the *worst* damn spy, in fact, because instead of leaving, I crept closer to his sleeping form.

I knew I shouldn't, I knew it was a terrible idea, but I couldn't stop myself. I felt pulled toward him, like a princess in a fairy tale drawn toward something clearly sinister but beautiful for all that.

He was my enchanted rose, my cursed spinning wheel, my shiny, poisonous apple.

All I wanted was to take a bite, even though it might kill me.

He was still mostly in shadow, but the moonlight revealed enough. His sharp mouth was softer now, parted as he breathed, and his thick hair was sticking in every direction in a mess of platinum silk. His sheet and blankets had pulled down to his stomach and his top half was bare. Lean muscles moved under his skin as he tossed and turned, his eyelashes fluttering on his flushed cheeks.

He mumbled my name again, in a throaty,

choked voice. "*Sloane*."

I held my breath, freezing again, but his eyes didn't open. He didn't say anything else. His chest still rose and fell with deep but slightly fitful breaths.

He was dreaming of me.

That sent a hard, hot thrum down every nerve I had, as if someone had shot lightning down my spinal cord. My fingers tingled, my face tingled. Everything prickled and sparkled with—I didn't know actually. Pleasure? Fear? Nervousness?

All three?

He stirred again, the blankets pulling so low on his waist that I could see his navel, and in the moonlight, the line of slightly darker gold that led from his navel down to where his hand . . .

Jesus, Mary and Joseph. He's jerking off. In his sleep.

Those long, elegant fingers were wrapped around himself, and I could see now that every twist and turn I'd attributed to mere restless sleep was actually something much filthier. His hips rolled, his back arched. His stomach rippled and tightened, and I could see at the bottom of the bed how his bare feet flexed and then slid under the covers as he fucked his own fist in his sleep. As he dreamed of me.

My body responded precisely as it had every time Lennox's cock—or fingers—or mouth—or mere proximity—had entered my awareness, and a hot, edgy knot began tying itself somewhere between my legs. Goosebumps erupted everywhere on my skin, and my mouth started watering. If my body called the shots, I'd already be kicking off my boots and jumping into his bed vagina-first.

But luckily I had more control than that. Enough control to realize that Lennox could never, ever know that I saw this. This was so much more private than a laptop and some emails. This was something I knew he would never forgive me for seeing. This was naked want—no walls, no weapons.

Just desire.

And I felt exactly the same. If only I could join him, skin to skin, mouth to mouth, fingers moving together . . .

"Beautiful," he murmured sleepily, and the word felt like sparks all over my skin. "So fucking beautiful."

Beautiful. Not hot. Not even *pretty.*

Oh my god. Oh my god. Was I sure he was dreaming of *me* still? But then he said something that obliterated all my doubts—and also reminded me that this wasn't a fairy prince at all, but Lennox Lincoln-Ward instead. "Suck me," he whispered as he twisted and moved his hand down his length. "Oh my god, suck me. Feels so good. So bloody good."

The accented words disappeared into sleepy mumbles as he continued to writhe and arch, one long leg getting tangled out of the covers as he rolled to his side and pressed his cock against a pillow. *That* seemed to be even better for him, and his breaths came in short bursts as his hips surged against the soft material. Because of the way the covers were rucked up, I could see the hollow at the side of his ass. I could see how the lean but powerful muscles bunched and flexed as he rocked his dick forward.

And because of how big that wonderful dick was, I could see the thick, flushed crown of it surging forward every time he moved.

"Yes," he mumbled again. "Fuck. Waited forever."

Me too, I thought, half-miserably. *Me too.*

The sparks across my skin were roaring bon-fires now. The heat between my legs could melt whatever they tiled space shuttles with. I wanted to watch the rest. I wanted to see what happened when that thick erection finally throbbed and pulsed out its release. I wanted to see Lennox's face as the pleasure of it moved through him.

I wanted it all.

And I could have nothing.

All of this was wrong as hell, and I had to leave before I did something irrevocably stupid, something that couldn't be undone.

And so with a hard swallow and a wince as my entire core protested this new plan of action, I crept quietly to the window. And there I made my escape, climbing back out into the cold and dropping into the quiet, foggy night.

Chapter Eight

Sloane

I HADN'T SLEPT. The small external drive I'd used to copy Lennox's files and the letter I'd stolen had burned a hole in my pocket.

I tossed again and punched my pillow.

You don't have feelings or emotions. Control this. Get over it.

The problem was, there was no way I was ever going to get over watching Lennox Lincoln-Ward wrap that big hand of his around his, let's be honest, *enormous* dick and stroke. I will never forget the way my name sounded on his lips. I will never forget how he whispered, '*You're so beautiful.*' I will never forget the way he groaned as he begged imaginary me to suck it.

The other thing I would also never forget was how my entire body flushed like I'd been lit on fire from the inside as I was standing there holding a letter I shouldn't have been holding, and unfortunately having a bird's eye view of his hand on his dick.

You are so beautiful.

But that wasn't true. Lennox didn't think I was beautiful. And also, I was pretty sure of the fact that I just wasn't beautiful. I was pleasant-looking enough, sure. I had interesting features. Almost too delicate, too fine. But I had a body like a boy. What the hell was beautiful about me?

Serafina was standardly gorgeous by all meters. Starting with her medium-brown skin tone with nary a blemish in sight for all the years I'd known her, add to that ridiculously high cheekbones, enormous almond-shaped eyes, to that mass of curls I would die for. And her body. . . . . Jesus. It was like the body of a runway model. She was tall and athletic, but curved in places where I could only *dream* about curves.

When we'd first met as freshmen, she was slightly coltish, had more gangly arms and legs than anything. But now, she had turned into this complete and total knockout. She also possessed this unwavering confidence. I was her friend, so I knew that most of that was a complete lack of interest in what other people's opinions of her were. She knew who she was, and she didn't care what people had to say about her. But also, it was as if she didn't even see her own beauty. Like she somehow woke up every day and overlooked it.

She'd put on the adornments. . . . . Earrings. Makeup. And all that other shit. She didn't even need lashes. How is that fair? But she didn't revel in it. She could take or leave makeup. Take or leave the pretty trappings of patriarchal beauty. She didn't need it and she didn't care. She did it for her when she felt like it and because she liked it. And that's why I love her.

Then, of course, there was Aurora, the princess with the golden hair and the golden eyes. Well, black hair now since last summer. She practically screamed 'I'm a fairy princess, everyone should take care of me.'

That wasn't fair either, because Aurora was kind and generous. But if crossed, dear God help you. Which, of course, I respected. She had that inner core strength thing going for her. Her main motto was, 'do no harm, but take no shit', and that's why we were friends. But when your two best friends are complete stunners, it can get real complex.

My bedside clock said six-thirty, and I knew I didn't have to be up for another hour. But tonight was the gala, so I assumed Serafina and Aurora were going to kidnap me and make me try on dresses. I had tried to explain to Serafina about this gorgeous Howie pantsuit that I had, but she just stared at me. She said she had just the dress. She had yet to show me this dress, so I was slightly concerned. But I knew Sera, if she had made the decision, I was going to end up complying one way or another. With a groan, I sat up slowly, mindful not to wake her. She was still snoring heavily. Careful not to make noise, I pulled open the drawer by my bedside and took out my little locked box. I put in the code and then opened it gently. I took the external hard drive out then headed over to my desk to open my computer, plugged it in, and opened up an email to my father. I typed quickly. *"I've put on the encrypted server the files you requested."* Then I hit send, making sure all the files had, in fact, moved over to the encrypted server he'd set up for us to be able to send any sensitive documents. It was done.

No, it's not.

There was one thing I hadn't sent over. I could take a picture with my phone and easily send it, but something held me back. The *letter*, I wasn't sure what it was yet.

Are you really going to keep this from your fa-

ther?

No. Of course I was going to share it. Just not right now. I, at the very least, wanted to know more about what it was, or what I was dealing with before just blindly handing it over, because maybe it had nothing to do with any of us.

And also maybe you shouldn't have done it.

That was at the core of it. Up until I had heard Lennox whisper how beautiful he thought I was, I'd had some reservations about what I was doing. But my father's request had far outweighed those. However, after Lennox's whispered words, after knowing that I wasn't the only one who surreptitiously watched the other sometimes, after knowing that all his cruelty was directed at me because he felt something he didn't want to feel, that knowledge had changed how I felt about myself for taking that information.

I felt sick. Like there was some invisible line I had crossed, and I couldn't go back. Which is ridiculous though, because there are many lines I would cross for my family. But there are also ones that I wouldn't. I had my integrity. The ends had to justify the means, and I believed in justice.

Is this justice?

Lennox's father was the worst kind of greedy asshole. He'd stolen billions from unsuspecting people. The question was, was Lennox like that? Did he know what his father had done? Was he in some way an accomplice? My father would figure it out. My part was done.

Except for the letter.

I scrubbed a hand on my face, gathered the drive and put it back in my lock box, and then back in my top drawer. I would think about this another time. I'd done enough damage for the day, hadn't I?

I tried to climb onto the bed, hoping now that I'd handed the information over, I could at least get another hour of sleep. But suddenly, Serafina dragged the covers off and sat up. "Oh no, you don't. You're not going back to bed. We have a long day ahead of us."

I groaned. "Yeah, I have a couple of projects I want to get a head start on. And then I should answer some emails, and I have some errands to run before we drive down."

Serafina just gawked at me. "No. You're not doing any of that."

I frowned. "What? I do have errands to run. I have a lot of stuff I need to do before the gala tonight."

She shook her head. "You are going to take care of those errands tomorrow. The only thing you're doing right now is trying to get ready for the gala."

I frowned. "Sera, you know that that's not until seven o'clock tonight. And even with the drive, there's no way I need *that* much time. I promise, I'll get ready around two or three? Quick shower—I'll even work on putting on some good eyeliner."

I wasn't bad with makeup, when I bothered to try. I wasn't some YouTube influencer, but when I put on makeup, I liked to think I looked presentable. Well mostly, I could do some mascara and some lashes. I never had figured out contouring or any of that nonsense. But basic concealer, powder and the eyes, I could do that.

Serafina just shook her head. "My god, how can I love one person so much, and still watch her be a daft cow—as Aurora would put it. This isn't just a 'hey, we're getting ready to go out with the team, half makeup' kind of situation. You need to be scrubbed and exfoliated from head to toe."

I laughed. "No, I don't. I promise. I mean, I'm going to shower."

Sera just rolled her eyes and went to her closet, yanking it open. When she reached in to grab a zipper bag, I frowned. "What's that?"

"*This*, Sloane, is your dress." She marched

over wearing her cut-off tee that said, 'my brain is bigger than your brain' right across her boobs, and what looked like boys' boxers. She laid the dress on my bed and then proceeded to unzip. The gorgeous teal fabric had me gasping. "Oh, the color is so pretty."

"I know, right? The moment I saw it, I thought of you. It's going to bring out the green in your eyes."

Even I could see the dress was perfect for me. A corset-y bit to make the most of my athletic curves, a slinky skirt to flatter my long legs. But the best part was, it had a slit. Two actually. So I'd be able to walk in it, and it wouldn't hinder my movements. I lifted my head and grinned up at her. "Oh, I love you, I think."

She laughed. "Uh, I know I'm loveable."

"You are loveable, but really, do we have to do the whole beautifying thing?"

She nodded. "Aurora is going to be here any minute. We're going to start the basics here and then we're headed to the spa."

I blinked once. Then again. "A what?"

She laughed. "Honey, I love you. You're a complete and total badass, but the fact that these girly places freak you the fuck out, we *have* to get that fixed. The manis and pedis are in order. A facial, an all-over body scrub. We're getting the works, babe."

"I don't need it. I don't need a scrub."

She ignored my protests and continued rattling off the treatments I was going to get.

"But I don't want treatments. I just— honestly, I don't really need that. Plus, I can't really afford any of that. I'm sure it's very expensive."

Serafina whirled on me and lifted a brow, then crossed her arms over her shirt. "Are you serious right now?"

"Look, I know you've gone through a lot of trouble, and I appreciate it. I do. But I don't need this. I—"

"It's a gift. You're my bestie, I'd rather have your company than not, and Tannith isn't here for me to spoil, so I have a lot of spoiling built up right now. So, you're coming whether you like it or not. Besides, my mother owns that spa. So treatments are free anyway."

I sighed. "Jesus Christ, there's no way I'm getting out of this, is there?"

She laughed. "No, there's no way. Besides, you're going to have Rhys and Lennox eating out of the palm of your hand."

"I don't want anyone eating out of my hand.

Besides, you feed a stray once and they'll never leave you alone." I slid her a glance. "What about you? Will a certain Harvard sophomore be in attendance tonight? I know he's been sniffing around." Bryce Kessler was the oldest son of Jeffry Kessler, the actor. He'd graduated two years ago and had always had a thing for Sera. She, on the other hand, had always kept him at arm's length.

"I'm not worried if he shows or not."

"Oh c'mon. I know you've been talking to him on the phone sometimes."

Sera always played things close to the vest when it came down to her personal feelings. "Sure, we talk. But he's not my boyfriend or anything. Hell, I'm not sure I'll ever let him take me on a date. I like to assess the whole field before making a choice. Dating is a game of chess and not checkers. Best not to move too quickly. Besides, Rhys hates him. So son of an actor or not, no way he's welcome."

The way she said Rhys's name made me flush. "Serafina, you're okay with me going with him, right?"

She blinked wide eyes at me. "Yeah, I'm totally fine with it."

"Are you sure? Because I know you and Rhys have a—" How the hell should I even classify their thing? It was intense loathing, followed by an 'I will kill you in your sleep' vibe.

"Honey, I know you're not super into him. And also, I just don't care. He can date whoever he wants."

"We're not dating."

"You're kissing and making out on occasion, that spells *dating* to me." She waved her hand, dismissing the topic. "Honestly, I'm good. I love you. And if you think Rhys can make you happy, then fine."

"Oh, my god, Rhys does *not* make me happy. And let's be really clear, I don't think he'd make me happy. For some reason, I'm interesting to him at the moment, and I'm not sure why. He's probably just bored with nothing else to do, spotted me and decided I'd be the apple of his eye for the time being. In my case, I figured he'd make a good practice boyfriend, so here we are."

Serafina lifted her brows. "What?"

"I mean look, I know Rhys isn't really interested in me. Why he is trying to hang out with me, I'm not sure. But he is . . . well, he is a very good kisser. I sort of feel a little warm and tingly when he kisses me, although not that fireworks-exploding kind of shit like with—"

I cut myself off before I said too much.

She lifted a brow. "Like with who?"

"Wow, look at this dress, isn't that—"

She shook her head. "Don't you dare try to change the subject. Like with who?"

I swallowed hard. "Like with Lennox."

Her eyes went wide. "I knew it. Did you ask Rhys to kiss you to make him jealous?"

I frowned at that. "No, I wouldn't do that. I don't want to play games."

She sighed. "Yeah, I know. That's not you. You're really direct and straightforward. But I knew there was something going on with you two."

"There's nothing going on with *us two*."

She folded her arms again, settling on her chest. "Oh yeah? Then tell me what happened when I saw him dragging you to a supply closet the other day?"

I opened my mouth to say something but decided otherwise. Then I opened it a second time, but then closed it again. I made another attempt trying to find just the right words, but it never came. Then on my fourth attempt, I just sighed. "You saw that?"

"Yes. Spill girl, spill."

"It wasn't—I don't even know how it happened. He dragged me in there and told me Rhys was the bad guy and I couldn't date him. And then he asked me to go to the gala with him instead."

Serafina laughed. "Oh my god. You are the cutest innocent badass vixen ever."

"I don't even know what that means."

"It just means that you're not even trying, and you have these guys falling all over themselves for you. Please, teach me your ways."

I gave her the once over. "You and I both know full well, all you have to do is give somebody the time of the day, and he's at your feet. *You* have this quality that just says, 'I'm badass and sexy'. *I* don't have that quality. I just have the badass and scary vibe which I cultivate, and I'm good with, but that's just it."

"I think you need to see yourself differently. And we're going to do that today. Because I don't think you see yourself clearly enough."

I opened my mouth to argue, but Serafina held up a hand. "Nope. I have spoken."

I laughed. "I'm going to regret this whole day, aren't I?"

She grinned. "Yes, you are. But also you're going to look like a total bombshell. You're going to see *you* properly for the first time. I promise."

Maybe it was because she said it, or maybe it

was that fierce glint in her eyes. Maybe it was just because I wanted to. But for some reason, I believed every word out of Serafina's mouth.

CHAPTER NINE

LENNOX

THE PROBLEM WITH benefit galas was, by and large, unless you snuck off with your mates, there was nothing to drink. No one cared that at eighteen, in UK, or anywhere else in Europe for that matter, I'd be able to drink. No, I was relegated to soda water. Or Cokes. Or ginger beer. And right now, I needed a fucking drink or I was going to lose my mind.

Where the hell was she? I kept looking for flickers of her slicked-back hair, glimpses of her bright green eyes. I could almost guarantee she'd be wearing some kind of pantsuit, or maybe something fitted and tight. *You never did know with Sloane.*

She was always a little edgy, in an understated way, but she liked to be comfortable and she liked to be able to move. It was always strange talking to her, like she was looking for the exits. I knew for a fact she'd grown up—while not as wealthy as most of us—entirely comfortable. So why did she always feel the need to be so guarded? So afraid?

Why do you care?

I didn't.

I was in luck. Some geezer had left behind his scotch as he'd gone to dance. I could easily liberate him from this.

I grabbed the glass of the untouched drink and smiled to myself. "Sometimes it's just too easy."

On the dance floor, I caught sight of Serafina and my twin totally enjoying themselves. Aurora was in a short frilly-looking pink tulle dress of some sort.

And Serafina . . . Oh god, Serafina, she was in some white and mint-colored ensemble. It was sleek. Elegant. Maybe I *should* turn my attention towards her.

Serafina had the benefit of being a girl who didn't hate me, *and* it would piss off Rhys.

Although, I'd never really imagined that Serafina would give me the time of day. She was always nice enough. Had no real problems with me. But she didn't seek me out or look at me like most of the other girls at school did.

The last thing you need is to chase a woman who clearly doesn't want you.

Maybe she would. I knew what I looked like. More than half of the girls at school had indicated they'd love to try it on. Not her though. And come to think of it, I'd never seen her with a boyfriend. Maybe she wasn't into guys.

I could always just ask around to see what she's like.

Or, you could wait for a woman you actually want.

My gaze raked over Serafina once again. She was absolutely stunning. And I'd be lucky to have her in my bed. Hell, I was half hard just thinking about it. The problem was, she didn't make my skin itch. She didn't make me want to crawl out of my own skin. She didn't make me want to roar or howl at the moon, or whatever the hell that was. She didn't make me crazy. That was all *Sloane.*

Where the hell *was* she? The three of them were attached at the hips—even more so after Tannith went to Los Angeles and Iris went to Paris. So, if Sera and my twin were together without her, someone must have dragged Sloane off somewhere.

And I knew who that someone was.

I watched as Aurora gently tapped Serafina's arm with her hand. And then Sera turned towards the stairs. A wide grin spread across her face, making her appear even more stunning and regal. I turned to see what she was looking at, and I gasped. At the top of the stairs was Rhys in an excellent Oswald Boateng suit. On his arm was the girl I'd been waiting for practically my whole damn life. She was with him, and it made me want to kill someone.

My gaze homed in on her. She was wearing a teal-green dress. The top part looked like some kind of a cap sleeve corset or something. I don't really understand how the dress worked, but it somehow made Sloane look like she had curves. *Full ones.* It took whatever boobs she did have and encased them in some silk and shoved them up under her chin. I wanted to lick them.

Easy does it. You can't go sporting the goods at a gala.

The rest of the dress hugged her figure expertly, flaring slightly at her hips. It had slits that went all the way up to her thighs, allowing her freedom of movement. Her hair was down instead of pulled back in her characteristic short ponytail. It hung free and loose with a little more body than usual. Slightly curled. Her hair came to her chin, more to one side of her face. She looked stunning. Pity she was being escorted by a shit-eating, smirk-faced Rhys.

Suddenly, Owen appeared at my side. "You good? You're not going to do anything daft, are you?"

I drained the rest of the scotch. It went down smooth, warming up my belly when it hit. "I feel fine."

"Are you sure about that?"

"I mean, my desire to kill him is only . . . I'd say at an eight instead of a ten from the other day. So count that as progress, mate."

Owen chuckled low. "You two have got to figure it out, bro. Are you really going to lose your shit over a girl?"

"What would you know about it?" I grumbled. Owen never lost control. Girls flocked to him and then he dismissed them when he was done.

But interestingly, Owen's grip tightened around his glass, and something hungry and possessive flared in his eyes.

"I'm learning something about it," he muttered darkly, taking a drink.

I stared at him. "Is there something you'd like to tell me?"

"Nothing to tell. I'm Owen Montgomery, and I'll get what I want eventually. She won't say no to me."

"Who is *she*? Does she go to Pembroke?"

Owen actually bared his teeth. "None of your fucking business, twat."

"Goddamn but you are really twisted up over this girl," I said. "I never thought I'd see our Ice King brought so low as to have human feelings."

"They're not *feelings*," he bit out. "And I'm not twisted up. I know exactly what I want, and I have no doubt she'll give it to me. Unlike you, I don't let a random girl fuck with my plans. Or my friendships."

Owen really should know better. Sloane wasn't just *any* girl. She was mine. And the fact that Rhys was getting that pleasure right now pissed me off. Beyond Sloane being mine, he could say or do something to really damage her. At least I knew when to stop. I had drawn some lines I would not cross.

It was a delicate balance, and I didn't think Rhys had that line.

Owen's voice was a low whisper. "Look, just let her go. If you didn't do anything about wanting her all this time, don't be cheesed off that he's doing something about it. And don't let it

BECKER GRAY

fuck with your friendship. Definitely don't let it fuck with Hellfire."

"What would you do? If Rhys was planning to stick his tongue in your mystery girl's mouth?"

Owen didn't answer, but he didn't need to. The cold, murderous flare in his eyes was answer enough. Whoever this mystery girl was, Owen wasn't about to let her go.

"If he hurts Sloane," I said, "I will rip his fucking cock off and peel it. Mate or no mate, Hellfire or no Hellfire."

Owen whistled low. "Wow, thanks for the visual. I really needed that."

Across the room, I watched as Rhys led Sloane to the dance floor, and I caught myself grinding my teeth. *That fucking arsehole.*

I sat the glass back down on the bar top and then glanced around the crowd looking for Sera. She had moved from her last position. When I found her in the corner talking to Aurora, I stalked over. "Ladies." Aurora gave me a quick glance over and a small smile. But I knew only one girl would have the desired effect. "Serafina, what do you say we dance?"

She lifted a brow. "Well, can you dance, Lennox?"

I clasped my hand to my chest as if horrified

she would ask such a question. "I will have you know that royalty are taught to dance at a very young age. I shall not embarrass you."

She shrugged. "Sure, why not? Let's see what moves you have."

I led her to the dance floor, making sure we were standing three feet away from Rhys and Sloane, and then I twirled Serafina in my arms. She giggled. Her laugh was light but throaty and it made me smile. I mean, hell, what was I doing chasing a girl I wasn't sure I liked when I had one I knew I liked right in front of me? She was beautiful. Brilliant. Ridiculously wealthy. And she had the kind of name nobody could sniff at. She was a god damn *van Doren*. I should want to date her. And she did have very nice lips.

As we danced, I tried to picture myself kissing her. And I imagined her staring at me with longing in her dark eyes, but then she lifted a brow asking me what the fuck I was doing.

I had to bite back a laugh as I pulled her close.

"A little close, aren't you, Lincoln-Ward?"

"It is a dance, after all, van Doren."

She pulled back with a smirk. "I don't think you and I have ever been this close."

I glanced over her shoulder at Rhys, who was holding Sloane far too close. Wanker looked like

BECKER GRAY

he was trying to kiss her.

"Well, to dance, you have to get close. It's like the Zayn song; *I just want to get closer.*"

She laughed this time. A deeper and throatier one. And I was momentarily stunned. God, she really should laugh more, but I wasn't going to be the insensitive arsehole who would suggest that.

As we danced, she proved a fantastic partner. She not only knew how to dance, but also she took gentle leads well. It was effortless. So simple.

But my gaze over her shoulder was trained on Rhys and Sloane, and then that motherfucker kissed her. His eyes locked with mine as he leaned in and kissed Sloane nice and slow. Like she deserved to be kissed.

My throat constricted. I knew the one thing that would have set him off. The one thing that would have him releasing what was mine. I flicked my gaze to Sera's and she lifted a brow. "What are you looking at me like that for?"

"Is there a reason why you and I have never gone out?"

She laughed. "There are several reasons why. Are you looking for just one? I could do a whole dissertation."

"Ouch, I'm not that bad."

"No. You're not that bad. I don't know. It

wasn't meant to be, I guess."

"Maybe we should change that." I leaned in close, and she snapped her head back.

"If you put your tongue anywhere near me, I will bite it off."

My jaw unhinged. "You don't want me to kiss you? I thought we were having fun."

"Yes, we're having fun. And I'm not going to lie; you are very pretty to look at. The hair, the eyes, and you have very sexy lips. But I prefer to be kissed by people who *want* to kiss me. I'm nobody's substitute. I wouldn't stand for it. And frankly I'm disappointed you think I would . . . or should. Is that what you think, fuck face?"

Fuck. "I—I'm sorry. That was shitty. I'm a wanker."

She shook her head. "Oh my god, you're such a loser. If you want her, go and get her. Don't let Rhys fuck with her head. I know she's brilliant and amazing, but he doesn't. I'm pretty sure if you actually stepped up and weren't a dickhead to her, she might actually like you."

My gaze flickered to the happy kissing couple on the dance floor and a gnawing hunger churned my gut. "You know what? You're right. I'm fucking done with this."

She patted my arm. "Well then go do something about it. I'm tired of watching that shit show too." I gave her arm a quick squeeze before I released her and marched over to Rhys and Sloane.

When I reached them, I tapped on Rhys's shoulder. He lifted his hand and snarled at me. "Fuck off."

"I'm cutting in, mate."

Sloane's brows knitted together. "What in the world are you doing?"

"What I should have done a long time ago."

Rhys rolled his shoulders. "If you want to tussle again, we can do that. I'm not letting her go. Why should I just give her to you?"

"She's not yours, Rhys. She never fucking was."

I took Sloane's hand. She tried to fight me on it. "What the fuck do you think you're doing? Everyone is *staring*."

"I'm sorry. I'm going to apologize for this now. You can kick my arse for the next part later."

"Kick your ass for what?"

With the palm of my hand, I shoved Rhys away from her, and then I bent down, picked her up and tossed her over my shoulder. "You and I are going to talk. Rhys isn't bloody invited."

With the whole gala staring at us, and with

Sloane slumped over my back doing her level best to fight her way free, I marched out of that ballroom.

CHAPTER TEN

SLOANE

TO SAY THE Huntington mansion was large would be like saying being gutted with a fish hook stings a little. The mansion had a footprint bigger than most national museums, with grounds that stretched for acres and acres, sloping all the way down to a cold and crashing sea.

And I was currently being hauled like a Viking captive across *all of it*.

Well, maybe not all of it, but close enough. Lennox carried me, struggling and twisting atop his shoulder, out of the ballroom, and through another arched room strung with fall foliage and thousands of twinkling lights. It was also filled with people talking, mingling, drinking, and not one of them stopped to help me, even though I was clearly being hauled off against my will. No one hardly even *looked* at me, and when they did, their eyes would slide over to the famous white of Lennox's hair and they'd give me an apologetic sort of look. As if to say: *I couldn't possibly stop a prince, you understand, don't you?*

Rich people were absolute garbage.

Except then, I realized—belatedly and only as we walked through a set of massive doors and onto a breeze-buffeted portico outside—that I'd been smiling.

Smiling!

Fuck, no wonder no one had helped. I must have seemed positively gleeful to be perched atop the tuxedoed prince's shoulder.

"Lennox, put me down," I said, as authoritatively as I could. "Or take me back to the portico."

His arm was banded around the back of my thighs, and it tightened, as if even the idea of letting me go pissed him off. "If I put you down, then I'm tearing your dress off right here on the steps, darling."

He made the word *darling* sound like the angriest and filthiest word in the English language. "And it's not a portico," he added, "it's a loggia."

"And you're not a prince, you're a *prick*. Put me down."

"No."

"I mean it, Lennox."

"Or what? You'll hurt me? We both know if you truly wanted to be off my shoulder, you would be in a heartbeat." He was taking the shallow steps two at a time down to the moonlit lawn, away from the house and towards the sprawling hedge maze that stood between the mansion and the sea. "But you don't want to be off my shoulder, do you?"

"I do," I said, but it came out weak even to my ears. He was right; if I'd really wanted out of his hold, I would have been out by now. I knew at least seven different ways to get down from here—four of them wouldn't even require any strength or particular skill at all, only speed.

So why was I still here? Why was I barely able to keep that smile off my face? Why did I want him to make good on his threat and rip my dress right off me?

Lennox's shoes crunched on the crushed gravel of the path as we walked away from the house.

"You're not going to throw me into the ocean, are you?"

His voice dripped with scorn when he answered. "Don't be ridiculous."

"Don't be ridic—you have me over your

shoulder like a caveman! Or a Viking! Or a Viking caveman!"

"And what do you think Vikings did with their beautiful captives, Sloane? Do you think they threw them into the ocean?"

There was that word again. *Beautiful.* Something hot and dangerous bloomed in my chest to match the hot and dangerous thing already pulsing between my legs.

"Well, historically, yes," I managed to say, "some were probably sacrificed—"

"I'm not throwing you into the ocean," he interrupted coolly. "Although I have half a fucking mind to. I told you that you belonged to me, and I meant that shit." We were entering the maze now, Lennox's strides long and sure like he'd walked this path many times before. "Clearly you need to be reminded."

Familiar ire itched at me. "I already told you. I'm not yours." I kicked my legs to prove my point, which earned me a hard, fast slap on the bottom.

I should have shrieked. I should have pulled his hair or scratched his eyes out. Instead, I moaned.

Moaned.

I was becoming seriously unhinged over this

boy.

At the sound of my moan, Lennox's entire body stiffened under me. "How interesting," he said after a minute, his voice sneering and soft and fascinated. "I don't even need to have my fingers inside you to hear that noise."

Embarrassment flooded me everywhere. I *hated* that my desire for him could become a weapon in his hands. I *hated* that I didn't hate him . . . or that I didn't only hate him.

"Fuck you," I breathed. "Fuck you so much."

"Believe me, darling, I've thought about nothing else since the day we met," he said coldly. "Breaking you and fucking you. My twin obsessions."

"I could break you first."

"You could try. But we both know that the minute I touch your pussy, you sheathe those kitten claws for me, don't you? We both know I can make you come so good that it doesn't matter how much you hate me, you'll keep coming back."

I knew it was reckless when I opened my mouth, but I didn't care. I wanted to piss him off. I wanted him to be as angry as I was. "Maybe that's why I'm here tonight with Rhys. Maybe any Hellfire Club boy with long fingers will do, and I want to get my fix elsewhere."

Fury rippled through him, palpable and hot, and then he started walking even faster, muttering under his breath in his delicious accent. I could only catch a few words—*owed, mine, come*—but it was enough. Enough for me to know that whatever came next would be our biggest clash yet. Enough for me to know that he was serious as hell about me being his to torment and break, and he would stop at nothing when it came to wrecking me.

I WAS FREEZING by the time we got to the center of the Huntington maze. My dress was a gossamer-thin silk with barely any sleeves and two high slits up the front, which meant I was covered with goosebumps head to toe.

It also meant I felt the warmth of the fires before I saw them—dancing flames throwing light against the dark hedge walls. We were in the very heart of the maze now, approaching a stone structure that faintly resembled an ancient Greek temple—or at least, the idea of a Greek temple according to some Victorian-era Huntington who'd had too much money and not enough firsthand exposure to ancient architecture. Four braziers burned brightly at each of the corners, and the open spaces between columns were hung with curtains. Some were opaque, some were sheer, and they were all billowing gently in the breeze, parting just enough for me to make out a sunken fire in the middle surrounded by cushions and pillows and blankets. It was a space clearly meant for leisure and relaxing.

Or sex. Because everything about it—from the fires to the silk curtains to the cushions—screamed *do immoral deeds here!*

Which was exactly what I suspected Lennox had in mind.

Lennox mounted the stone steps into the open-air room and finally set me on my feet. For a brief instant, I considered running. I was in heels, yes, and I had very little practice running in them, but I had excellent balance, and anyway, I could always kick them off before I went. The slits in the dress would make for easy movement, and I'd noted every turn Lennox had taken in order to get here.

I could find my way out.

So why wasn't I running?

Lennox was closing the curtains from where we'd come in, and when he turned back toward me, his golden eyes were molten with raw anger and his mouth was the sharpest and cruelest I'd ever seen it.

"You fucked up coming here with Rhys, darling," he said, taking a step toward me. "You weren't his to bring."

"I keep *telling you*, I'm not anybody's."

Another step. "But that's not true, is it? I already own you. I have for years."

I shivered at his words. Because I hated them . . . or because they were true, I didn't know. I just know they made me feel like he already branded his initials on some tender, vital organ in me. Like my heart.

Why did he captivate me so much? Why did I smile when he carried me, why didn't I run away when I had the chance?

Was it that mouth? Those unnaturally beautiful eyes? The cruelty?

The challenge?

I didn't understand it, and I hated things I didn't understand. Dad always said it would be my biggest weakness in criminal justice: my hunt for the bigger reason, the *why* of it all.

Sins very rarely have an interesting motive, he'd told me once. *Lust, greed, ambition. Everything gets boiled down to something predictable in the end.*

"Why?" I asked Lennox now, knowing that I

wouldn't get a satisfying answer but needing to ask anyway. "Why this? Why us? Why did you decide I was yours? Why did you ever even notice me?"

He was in the middle of taking another step forward, and I could see my question surprised him a little. A faint line appeared between his brows. "I noticed you because you're you," he said, as if it were an indelibly obvious answer. "But as for being mine . . . well, I decided that once I heard your name."

"My name? But—"

"That's when I learned you were Nathan Lauder's daughter."

"Why—"

But I stopped myself, because I already knew why that mattered, didn't I? After three years of thinking it *couldn't* be the reason, here it had been all along, plain as day. Obvious to anyone with eyes.

Obvious to anyone who hadn't blindly trusted her father's lies.

My next words came out slowly, reluctantly dragged from somewhere deep in my throat. "Years ago, my dad told me he was only barely involved with your father's case, but's that's not true, is it? He finally told me this week. He was the one who made the arrest. He was the one who investigated your father."

I couldn't read Lennox's face or voice now; it was as if everything in him had gone flat. Dead. "Investigated is a kind word, Sloane. A very kind word."

"And what—I'm some sort of revenge plan? Because your dad was a criminal and my dad was a cop? I thought you *wanted* your father in prison—I know Aurora does—so how can you blame my father for putting him there? How can you blame *me*? Want *revenge* against me?"

A muscle jumped in his jaw, and he opened his mouth—and then closed it again. As if he'd changed his mind about what he was about to say.

Instead, he took another step forward. He was close enough to reach out and touch me now, though he didn't. Not yet.

It was strange, the disappointment I felt right then. All this time, I'd thought I'd somehow earned Lennox's hatred on my own. I thought we'd become mortal enemies because of some marrow-deep connection . . . some fated gravity between us.

But no.

The bullying, the torment, the stolen kisses . . . it was all about a years-old grudge. Despite what I'd believed—what I'd foolishly *chosen* to believe—it was about my father all along. Not about me at all.

I was completely irrelevant.

"It doesn't matter how it started," Lennox finally said. "We're still going to finish it."

I looked up at him, feeling dull and teary. But I did everything I could to blink the tears back. He hadn't made me cry in four years, and I wasn't going to give him the satisfaction now.

I had to go. I needed space away from him, from us, from this toxic bloom that was our fascination with each other.

"There's no finish for us, Lennox. I don't know what this is—" the words left me in a choked breath "—but it's over now. Goodbye."

I made to step around him, but his hand shot out to grab mine and his eyes shifted then, going from winter sun to blazing summer light. "Don't go," he said, and there was something wild in his voice, something that wasn't cold or cruel at all. "Please. Don't go yet."

I looked down at where he held me. He wasn't holding my arm or my wrist. He wasn't gripping me with any real strength. Not because he didn't care if I left—I could practically feel him vibrating with how much he cared—but because he was *asking*.

For the first time, ever, Lennox Lincoln-Ward was asking for something.

"We both know you can fight me," he continued, bending his knees a little so he could catch my gaze. "We both know you can fend me off, beat me down, kill me if you have to. So stay, Sloane. Don't go. You know I can't really hurt you."

"You should know," I tell him, pulling my arm free and glaring, "that there are more ways to hurt a person than only with their body."

"Then hurt me for every time I hurt you. Kick me when I sneer. Punch me when I taunt. I don't care, *just stay*."

Misery shimmered through me like waves over hot asphalt. "I don't want to kick you or punch you, Lennox. All I've ever wanted is for you to leave me alone."

The wildness was still in his face and voice when he reached for me again. "I won't, I won't leave you alone, not ever—"

His fingers made contact with my wrist and something snapped in me. Something that was more than anger, something that was worse than embarrassment.

Hurt.

The outside edge of my free hand came down hard on his wrist, loosening his grip, and then I shoved him back, hard enough to make him stagger a step or two backwards. It felt so good that I did it again, and again, shoving and shoving him until he was practically in the fire pit. Shoving him until my body was hot with something other than hurt, until my hand was fisted in the lapel of his tuxedo, and my nipples were hard enough to bead against the silk of my dress.

"Do it until you feel better," he said, his voice ragged and his breaths coming fast. "Hurt me as much as you want."

"I'd have to hurt you for a thousand years to make up for all the things you've done to me," I whispered, and his eyes were so gold right then, and his mouth was so gorgeous, and the fire gleamed all along those sharp cheekbones and that perfect jaw, and I hated him, I hated him, *I hated him—*

This time it was me seeking his mouth. This time it was me yanking him down to my lips and kissing him like I'd die if I didn't. Like the only way I could breathe was against his mouth, and the only air I could drag into my lungs was the air we breathed between desperate, hungry kisses.

CHAPTER ELEVEN

SLOANE

IT WAS HIS turn to shove now, and I was pushed right onto my back, like he really was a Viking intent on pillaging me. Except I didn't fall onto the ground, I fell onto a pile of luxurious cushions and blankets, and he was no Viking, but all prince, with his ten-thousand-dollar tuxedo and his white-gold hair falling into his eyes as he crawled over me.

"Go ahead," he breathed, "hurt me. Stop me. We both know you can."

I could. I could have him off me in a heartbeat. I could have him cupping his testicles and weeping. I could have him blinded and screaming.

But instead, I threaded my fingers into the white silk of his hair and pulled him down to my mouth again.

His kiss was as hot as his heart was cold, and

when his mouth opened over mine, a moan worked its way free from my throat. There was nothing like his kisses, nothing at all, nothing like that tongue slipping past my lips and stroking against my own. Nothing like the way he searched and plundered my mouth, seeking out all my secrets and all my lies.

An exquisite heat knotted between my legs, directly tied to the fluttering in my stomach and the ache in my breasts, and I parted my thighs, my hands finding his hips and pulling him closer. There was no argument from him, and the moment his tuxedo-clad erection pressed against my needy core, we both groaned.

Still he kissed me, still his mouth made me his own, but now he propped himself on one hand as his other hand slid up my leg. One of the dress's slits had opened around my thigh, and so my leg was completely bare and exposed to the chill of the night. The contrast between the cold air and his warm hand was enough to start my stomach fluttering all over again.

And then his hand moved between us, using the slit for its inevitable purpose.

"A thong," he murmured. "Have you ever worn a thong before, Sloane?"

His fingers traced around the edges of the

fabric as he talked. As thongs went, it wasn't meant to be sexy. It was a seamless thing meant to hug my body and prevent any lines from showing through the dress. It was functional and direct. Like me.

But when Lennox touched it, he made it feel like it was woven of the naughtiest lace and the purest sin. His fingers were shaking, and his pupils were so blown that his eyes were no longer gold, but black, with only a gilded ring around the outside.

His breathing was harsh. Ragged. Like this was the sexiest thing he could have ever imagined.

This is definitely the sexiest thing *I* could have ever imagined, with the possible exception of watching him jerk off in his sleep.

"No," I managed to say. "I've never worn one before."

"It's wet here," he said, the back of his knuckles brushing over my seam. I bit back a moan. "So wet. Did you feel naughty wearing this? Did you feel naughty knowing I'd inevitably see it?"

"Yes," I admitted. "*Yes.*"

He tugged at the fabric, causing it to press and pull against my swollen flesh. This time, I couldn't hold back the helpless noise I made.

"I want it off," he growled, his fingers now

curling around one side of it. "I want you completely bare for me."

It didn't even occur to me to argue. Why would it have? I wanted less between us too, I wanted *nothing* between me and his touch. I helped him pull the thong off, and I didn't even mind when he tucked them into the pocket of his tuxedo pants, as if he planned on keeping them. And then he kissed me fiercely, almost like a reward, and I was lost. Lost to his drugging kisses, lost to the feel of his hand roaming everywhere— cupping a breast, searching out a nipple, sliding to my hip and the slit in my dress and rubbing me until I was arching and gasping.

"Um, why are you—" His voice cracked. "Have you had a Brazilian?"

I groaned. "Oh my god, Serafina insisted when we did spa day. Can you imagine?"

He coughed a laugh. "Sort of. But I like it."

I bit his bottom lip. "Okay, it feels kind of amazing, actually. Your fingers on my bare skin."

"Who are you telling?" he growled.

I couldn't answer, I couldn't even think, because he was doing something to my clit that rendered all thoughts null and void. All I could do was lift my hips and pant.

"Every time," he breathed between kisses, his

hand lifting from my pussy to his fly. "Every time we do this, I get you there, and then you leave me so fucking hard up for it, Sloane. And I can't stand it. I spend hours tossing myself off after, and it's still not enough. I'm still miserable for days and days, and it kills me, it kills me."

My hands were everywhere too, unbuttoning his jacket and sliding up his stomach and pulling at his bow tie. "I'm miserable for days after too," I confessed. "You make me come, and then I want more and more, and it takes everything I have not to find you and beg you for it."

"Is that so, darling? All you've ever had to do was ask."

"Liar."

"I never lie about what's important. You belong to *me*. If this virgin cunt needs to come, then I'll be the one seeing to it. No one else. Not Rhys. Not anyone. Is that fucking clear?"

His bow tie was finally undone, hanging from his collar and tickling my throat. "Still jealous of Rhys?" I asked.

A scowl curved his mouth. "Yes, I'm still bloody jealous. I don't like it when other people touch my things."

My heart twisted a little as I remembered why he'd claimed me as his thing—not because he

wanted me, but because he resented my father—
but the feeling was quickly overridden by his
fingers between my legs again. Then his knuckles.
Brushing oh-so-gently against my naked skin.

"And I'm your thing?" I asked, arching against
his touch.

"My pretty, broken thing."

"I'm not broken yet," I reminded him, although the point seemed rather academic as I was
currently panting underneath him with my
panties in his pocket.

The scowl turned into a vicious smile. "You
will be."

And then I realized what the brushing of his
knuckles was: he'd been freeing himself from his
tuxedo pants. And now he impatiently shoved the
rest of my skirt out of the way so he could wedge
his erection against my pussy as he leaned in to
kiss me again.

We looked like a mess, a complete and decadent mess. Me with my gown up to my hips, him
with his tuxedo still on but his bow tie unknotted
and dangling.

And the way we *felt*—well, that was beyond
decadent. The hot, velvety skin of his thick length
pressed against me, the combination of silk and
expensive wool tangled everywhere, his firm lips

dragging over my mouth and jaw and throat.

He moved down to my breast, sucking my nipple through the silk bodice, and then back up to my mouth. Every time I moved, his swollen cock rubbed against my clit, sending bursts of pleasure rocketing through my core and sizzling all over my body.

"You're so fucking wet," he said, rocking against me. His thick inches spread me apart when he moved like that, made it so I got him even wetter. "You get so fucking wet when we fight, my darling. You get so fucking wet when I tell you all the ways you belong to me."

"I—don't belong—to—you—" The words came out as moans, as sighs, and we both knew them to be false. At the very least, they were false right now, as I was chasing his hips with mine, as I was kneading my clit against the erection he'd freed from his tuxedo.

And then it happened. We were tangled and arching and his teeth were scraping along my jaw, and suddenly the blunt, wide crown was pressed to my wet opening.

"Oh," I murmured, the different pressure sending frissons of need into my belly and thighs.

And at the same time, he muttered, "Christ, fucking Christ."

We didn't move for a moment, both of us absorbing the fact that his flesh was touching mine—*there*—the flared tip of his cock nudging against my hole. One thrust and he'd be inside me. Fucking my virginity away.

He lifted his head, his silky hair tumbling in his eyes, and stared down at me. His eyes were hooded, his lips swollen from kissing. "Let me," he said. "Let me."

He was trembling. His entire body was shaking. If I'd ever doubted that he wanted to have sex with me, then there were no doubts, not anymore. He was about to fly apart at the seams with how much he needed to shove himself inside me and fuck.

I was shaking too. My entire body screamed for this, for him; my thighs ached with the effort it took not to wrap around his hips and have him spread me open.

"You don't have a condom," I whispered foggily, trying to think. "We should have a condom."

"I'm clean," he said, dropping his forehead to mine. His breath was warm against my lips. "I'm clean. And we know you are. Are you on birth control?"

I shook my head under his.

He let out a ragged curse. "Ahh, fuck me, Sloane, the things I'm thinking right now . . ."

I moved my hips a little, swiveling on the head of his dick and shivering at how good it felt. "What things?"

"Fucked-up things. Filthy things."

"Like what?"

I could feel the tops of his thighs against the inside of my own, and I could feel how they flexed ever so slightly, pushing his crown just a little deeper. I gasped.

"Like I want to come inside you anyway," he murmured, kissing the side of my jaw and then nipping at my ear. "Like I want to pump you so full that you're leaking me down the inside of your thigh for the rest of the night."

Another flex of his hips, a tad bit deeper. He was still only barely inside me, but it was enough to pinch, enough to make me squirm with something that could have been pain or could have been pleasure, I wasn't sure which.

"I could fuck a baby into you," he purred into my ear. "I could keep you here all night, coming inside you over and over again. I could drag you back to my room at Pembroke and fuck you night after night until you were pregnant."

This shouldn't have been hot. I shouldn't

have been squirming even more at his fucked-up words. But I was. I was.

His hand came down between us, and he spread it wide over my stomach. "You like that, darling? You like how hot it makes me to think about fucking you without a condom?"

"I shouldn't," I said, which wasn't an answer, and he knew it.

I could feel his smirk as he took my hand and guided it down between us, directing my fingertips to trace the place where he was notched against me.

"That's the head," he said, as my fingers found the ridged crest at the top. "Now, here, circle me, just like that. You feel that throbbing? You feel how it jerks sometimes? That's for you. That's because I'm aching to sink deep inside you and fuck."

I shivered. I was aching for that too. "Really?"

His cock jolted in my hand, swelling even more. "Yes," he ground out.

"As revenge against my father?"

"Sure," he said. There was something evasive in his tone. "That's what it is."

I shouldn't have wanted him to go inside me bare—I had too much planned for my life to risk pregnancy—but something about it, about him claiming me in such a horribly primal way . . .

Well, it did make me wet. Something he felt, because he grunted, "I can feel you getting slicker, darling."

"I can't help it," I said, wanting *so badly* to have more of him inside me. "You mess with my head. You mess with everything. I hate you so much, but your cock feels so good—"

"Brilliant, because it's the only cock you're ever getting," he vowed. To underscore his words, he pushed his crown all the way in.

"*Lennox,*" I moaned. He was wide, so wide, invading my channel. He was maybe only an inch deep, but I felt him everywhere, my thighs and my belly and even in my chest.

"Shit," he mumbled, pressing his forehead to mine again. "I can't go any farther. That's your hymen stopping me."

He flexed his hips a little, moving back out and then again, as if to test the barrier. He was shivering, like he had a fever, and his forehead was burning hot against mine.

"I'm owed this, Sloane. I've been owed this for years. Your virgin pussy around my cock. Let me break your hymen, baby, please. Please. Please."

He was begging now. Wild. Like he'd been

every other time we'd fooled around—a bully and a prince brought utterly low by me, by the mere *idea* of fucking me.

It's revenge to him.

He doesn't care about you.

But I was so aroused, so frantic. Desperate for more and more and more. And even if I knew it was a lie, it felt like power to have him like this, to have him begging for something that I could so easily deny him.

God, it felt even better than power. It felt like its own kind of revenge, its own fucked-up victory.

Maybe that was what it would always be between us.

One of us pushing until the other broke.

"You can, but only if you make me come first—"

The words hadn't even finished leaving my mouth before his thumb found my clit, expertly circling and rubbing and pressing. "I could spend every waking minute making you come, Sloane. It's the only time you smile, did you know that? The only time I get to see your smile is when you're limp and shuddering from an orgasm I just gave you."

My head was thrashing on the pillow—I knew

my hair was going to be ruined and I didn't even care. It felt so good, so unimaginably good to have him working my clit with his cock inside me. With the thrilling potential that he could sink all the way in at any moment.

The climax was abrupt, sharp, wonderful. I dug my fingers into his hair and pulled him down to me as my orgasm broke against his talented touch, around the tip of his cock. I gasped into his ear as my cunt fluttered and fluttered and fluttered.

"Sloane," he rasped, and that was all. "Sloane."

He pushed against my hole and lifted his head to look down between us. I looked too, seeing the crude joining of him to me, seeing his thick erection pressing into me.

"I can feel you coming," he said in a tattered voice. "I can feel—it's so tight, Sloane. God, and knowing that I am the one who made you come—"

The climax was still rippling through me, but I wanted more, I wanted to fuck, I wanted Lennox to be the only thing that existed tonight. Him and his rough sex and the fire next to us and the sea roaring in the distance.

"Fuck me, Lennox," I pleaded. "I want it to

be you. I want you to be the first—"

"I'm going to be the *only*," he growled, and slid his arms underneath me.

I realized what he was doing; he was gathering me close, he was anchoring me so he could plunge in as hard as he needed, so he could shove past my virginity and fuck my whole pussy. There was the hard pulse of my orgasm still clamoring through me, there was the brutal pressure of his cock just barely wedged inside, and there was the feel of wool and silk tangled together, and then there was the smell of flowers and metal and the sound of the ocean—

And then I heard Lennox's name. Not from my lips, or from his, but from outside the temple folly, in the maze.

"Lennox?" a girl's voice called. "Lennox, are you in there?"

CHAPTER TWELVE

LENNOX

WE BOTH FROZE, looking at each other in a kind of lust-drunk panic. The kind of panic that says *maybe no one will notice us, maybe we can keep going, because we'll die if we can't keep going.*

At the very least, *I* would die. My erection gave a hard throb against her, arguing with me.

You're about to be all the way inside of Sloane Lauder's pussy, my cock shouted at me. *Nothing gets in the way of that.*

But then the voice called my name again, and we both recognized it at the same time.

Aurora. My twin and one of Sloane's best friends.

"Fuck," I said, but I didn't move. "Darling, I—"

"We have to get up," Sloane whispered.

"This isn't over," I said, in mortal agony. I propped myself on an elbow and looked down at the stern, beautiful face that haunted my dreams. "This is the furthest thing from over, Sloane."

"Okay, fine, it's not over—now get up or she'll see—"

I somehow managed to pull my cock free. How, I don't know, because it was the tightest, wettest thing I'd ever felt in my life. And it was virgin too, totally untouched except by me. As if she really had been waiting for me. As if I really had been owed her all these years.

Fuck. I'd been tossing off to this since the day I met her; my singular goal of making her life a living hell had somehow fused with the necessity of fucking her. And that had somehow fused with a possessiveness I couldn't explain even to myself.

She was mine. All fucking mine.

I wincingly closed up my tuxedo pants around my erection as Sloane attempted to rearrange her dress and hair. She held out her hand with her eyebrow raised.

"Panties, please."

I smirked at her. "It's cute that you think I'd even consider giving them back."

That earned me a typical Sloane scowl.

"Lennox?" I heard Aurora call again. Now

that my dick was back in my pants, I could hear the warble in my twin's voice.

Concern battled with my initial irritation at being interrupted. Aurora liked crying about as much as I did—which was to say, not at all. We hadn't cried when Dad was arrested or when our mother's humiliation was smeared all over the tabloids. We hadn't cried when we were sent off to boarding school.

We both had too much of that stupid Lincoln-Ward pride.

I helped Sloane to her feet—without asking her, by the way; I merely scooped her up and then set her down on her heels, which earned me another Sloane scowl. And then I pushed through the curtains separating the inside of the folly from the rest of the maze.

Aurora stood in front of the folly, shivering in her tiny, strapless gown. Her skin was covered in goosebumps, and her mascara was running down her cheeks and dripping off her jaw.

"Bloody hell, Rory, are you alright?" I asked, coming down the temple steps as fast as I could, Sloane right behind me. I shrugged out of my jacket and flung it over her shoulders, pulling it tight around her. "What the hell were you thinking coming outside like this? You'll freeze."

She sniffled. And then threw herself against my chest and started sobbing.

I held her tight, smoothing my hand over her back while I met Sloane's confused stare. That made two of us who were utterly lost as to what was happening.

"Did someone hurt you?" I asked, already growing angry at the thought. Aurora and I sparred plenty, but no one fucking hurt my twin, *no one*.

Aurora nodded tearfully against my chest, and I gently pushed her away from me, just enough so I could study her face and arms. If I saw any bruises, any scrapes, so help me God—

But there was nothing that I could see. Just her swollen lips and mussed hair.

"What happened?" I asked again, as softly as I could.

Her chin was dimpling, and I could see she had to swallow once or twice before she could force the words out. "Phineas," she whispered. "Phineas happened."

Phineas, that *fucking* playboy arsehole, I was going to kill him. I understood equal opportunity hatred very well—just look at Sloane and me—but whatever this was had crossed the goddamn line. Pleasant images of smashing his face with my fist danced in my mind, and given the way Sloane's scowl had curved into a darkly gleeful smile, I had to think she was imagining much the same thing.

"Let's get you inside," I said to my twin. "I know a place."

✧ ✧ ✧

TWENTY MINUTES LATER, we were in the Huntington kitchens, and I was getting a glass of water for my sister and a bottle of whiskey for myself.

I say kitchens *plural*, because the Huntington Mansion is old enough to have required hordes of servants and cooks back in the time before electric ranges and dishwashers, and so the kitchens are actually a cluster of rooms beneath the house, each room with a different purpose. There're pantries and larders and butteries and sculleries, and we were currently in an unused-for-decades scullery, close enough to the main kitchen that we could faintly hear the catering staff chattering and clattering dishes, but far enough away that we were hidden well out of view.

"How did you know this was here?" Sloane asked as I walked in with the water and whiskey. The water I handed Aurora, and the whiskey I unstoppered and took a swig of before I handed it to Sloane.

I expected her to fight me on it; I'd never seen her drink, not even once, but to my surprise, she grabbed the bottle by the neck and took a few healthy swallows.

"Rhys showed it to me," I said, taking a seat next to my sister. Sloane had found Aurora a blanket, and one of the reasons I'd chosen the scullery was because it had an old, clunky radiator that still worked, but Aurora was still shivering. I took the whiskey from Sloane and gave it to my twin. "Here, this will warm you up."

Aurora accepted it, her eyes hooded as she took several long drinks. Between the drama and the cold and getting warm again, I had the feeling she'd be asleep soon.

"Rhys knows where his scullery is?" Sloane sounded doubtful.

"More like he knows all the spots in his house where he can fuck someone without getting caught," I said, and then narrowed my eyes. "He might have tried to bring you down here, you know."

"He might have," Sloane agreed.

Jealousy rose in my blood again, so violent and sharp that I wanted to smash something.

"And would you have gone with him?"

Aurora was watching our exchange with the glazed listlessness of the almost-asleep. For her sake, I managed to keep myself from roaring and pounding my chest at the thought of Rhys touching what was mine.

It was Sloane's turn to narrow her eyes now. "Maybe."

"You're never going anywhere with him again," I said coldly. "If you go anywhere else like this, I'll be the one to take you."

Sloane's mouth tightened, but she didn't reply, turning away to smooth Aurora's messy hair with her hand instead. My sister sighed and then slid down to the floor, curling into a ball next to Sloane, her eyes already closing.

"What did he do, Rory?" Sloane asked softly, arranging my tuxedo jacket so it was a kind of pillow for her friend.

"What he always does," Aurora whispered. "He makes me think he cares, and I start to believe that he really does. And then I find him with his dick wet."

Sloane's free hand curled into a fist, but she didn't say anything. She merely kept stroking Aurora's hair, and within a few minutes, Aurora's soft snores filled the scullery. My sister was finally asleep.

Sloane got carefully to her feet, the slits in her dress showing off her leanly muscled legs as she did. Despite my sleeping sister only a few feet away, my cock surged to attention. I wanted to spend hours exploring those incredible legs of Sloane's. Tracing every muscle with my tongue.

"What are you doing?" I asked Sloane as she started opening drawers and cabinets at the far end of the scullery.

"Looking for knives," was the succinct answer I received.

"Er. Knives?"

Sloane turned and fixed me with a look that both made my cock hard as granite and also terrified the fuck out of me. *This* was the girl that made me finger her while she held her forearm to my throat. "Have you ever heard of a Colombian necktie?" she asked calmly.

"I—what?"

"I'm going to cut Phin's throat and then pull his lying, manwhore tongue through it."

I considered for a moment. Phin was my friend, but a Colombian necktie was about what he deserved after making my sister cry. "I'll help," I said. "Actually, I'll do it while you hold him down."

She glared at the empty cabinet in front of her, and then she slammed it shut with a bang. "I don't have time to teach you how to cut someone's throat, Lennox."

But there was something like a smile on her face when she turned to face me.

"Come here," I said from the floor, not sure what I was doing, but unable to stop. "Sloane, come here."

She hesitated for a moment, and then she walked over to me. I reached up and pulled her by the wrists so that she was straddling my lap. Next to us, Aurora continued to snore.

"What are you doing?" Sloane asked. "More to the point, what am I doing? I need to go kill Phineas."

"We'll kill him later," I murmured, looking up at her. It wasn't very bright in the scullery, because the only light came in from the doorway, and the shadows made her so very lovely. Almost like she was meant to be in them always. They turned her eyes dark and glossy, like mistletoe leaves in midwinter, and they set off her sharp jaw and her elegant cheekbones. They even traced her plush pout of a mouth—a sliver of shadow lingering under her full lower lip, a curl of shadow in the dip of her cupid's bow.

I extended my hand and traced her lips my-self, all the places where they curved and dipped. And then I pushed my finger past her lips and groaned in surprise when she sucked it. And then groaned again when she bit it.

Fuck, I was so hard.

I dropped my hands and ran them up her thighs—exposed by the slits in her dress—and then gripped her hips and pulled her firmly onto my lap, so that her cunt was against my erection.

"Oh," she said, her eyelids hooding as she felt me against her. She gave an experimental little rock against me and then shivered. "Okay," she whispered. "Okay, yes, we can kill Phineas later."

I let out a strangled laugh and then yanked her down to my mouth, kissing her like we were still alone in the folly. Kissing her like I still had her mounted.

Breaking our kiss, she looked over at Aurora, as if to reassure herself that Aurora was asleep still, and then she reached between us, hiking up her gown and fumbling for the fastenings of my trousers. I hissed the moment her fingers found me, throbbing into the cool air.

"This isn't because I care about you," my shadow-kissed tormenter said. "But fair's fair, and you've made me come so many times . . ."

I looked down at where she gripped me, her strong fingers wrapped around my shaft, the tuxedo and her silk gown rumpled between us, and then my head dropped back.

"Fuck," I mumbled. "*Fuuuck.*"

She moved her grip up and then down, slowly, as if testing it. Without moving my head, I looked at her. "Have you ever tossed someone off before?"

She shook her head. "Am I doing it wrong?" She moved her hand again, her fingers so strong and tight, and my toes curled in my patent leather Oxfords.

"No," I managed, my breath hitching. "Not wrong at all."

She gave me more strokes, a little tentative, but plenty tight, and my balls drew up close to my body, ready to release. It was almost embarrassing how little it was taking to get me there, but in my defense, this had been almost four years in the making. Four years of jerking off in my room alone.

And then she did something that will undoubtedly lead to four *more* years of jerking off. She let go of me and then shifted forward, until her bare cunt was on top of my dick, and started *moving.* Fisting her hands in my shirt and rocking over me, like she was giving me a handjob still, but with her pussy instead of her hands, and oh my god, oh my bloody god—

"You're so wet," I breathed, finding her hips and moving her over me harder, faster. "So wet. More. Fuck, give me more."

She widened her thighs and buried her face in my neck, letting me work her cunt over my erection, and it was so wet, so hot, and all I had to do was flex my hips just the right way and I could be inside her . . .

"Darling," I said in a choked murmur, "my sweet nothing, I'm going to come. I'm going to get you wet with it if you don't move."

"Do it, Lennox," she whispered against my throat. "Come all over me. I want to feel it on me."

That's all it took. I arched up, my thighs tense, my stomach rock-hard, and then for the first time, I came with Sloane Lauder. I came against her, *on* her, my cock throbbing jet after jet of hot fluid underneath her slick, wet cunt. I came and it spattered onto her, onto my dress shirt, making everything between us wetter and wetter. And every time she slid over me, I could feel the place where she opened. I could feel how close I was to heaven, and the knowledge made me come even harder.

I *would* be there. Soon. So fucking soon.

Sloane was mine, and tonight had proved it.

She gave a few small shudders against me as my pulses stilled and then slumped against my chest. I realized she'd been able to wring out an orgasm for herself too. I wrapped my arms around her and held her tight against me. Not because I wanted to be affectionate, obviously not.

Just . . . it felt better like this. My arms around her, her breath on my neck, our bodies still warm and wet and pressed together under her skirt.

"Seeing you with Aurora tonight . . . you're different than I thought you were," she murmured after a moment.

I ran my nose through her hair. Fuck, she smelled good. Like honeysuckle. Who knew the girl made entirely of knives and glares would smell like honeysuckle? "How am I different?" I asked idly.

"I don't know," she answered after a minute. "I guess I thought you were selfish, you know? Greedy."

Greedy. The word punched through me like a cannonball.

"Greedy," I repeated flatly. "Why would you

think that?"

She tried to sit up a little, and I let her. I wanted to see her face. "Why did you think I was selfish? Greedy?" I pushed. "Because of my father? Because your father told you that's what you should think of me?"

My voice was rising now, echoing off the walls of the scullery, but I didn't care. I didn't fucking care. It didn't matter what I did or who I did it for—it didn't matter how many years passed—I was always going to be my *fucking father* to the rest of the world.

Sloane regarded me warily. "You're extrapolating," she said in that quiet, clipped way of hers. "I never said any of that."

"You didn't fucking have to," I growled. "Get off me. Get off me right now."

A wounded look flashed over her face, and then it was gone before I could process what it really was or what it meant. She climbed off me and rose gracefully to her feet, adjusting her dress and checking on Aurora before walking to the door.

"Stay here with her," she said. "And then after she's awake, feel free to go fuck yourself."

CHAPTER THIRTEEN

SLOANE

MY HEAD SPUN.

How had everything gone so terribly wrong? How had I gone from writhing underneath Lennox in the maze—writhing on *top* of him in the scullery—to trying not to cry in Sera's limo on the way back to Pembroke?

Sera was wrapped in a cashmere blanket, dozing on her seat, and I was pretending to myself that I didn't have streaks of Lennox's orgasm painted on the inside of my thighs. I was pretending that I didn't want to curl into a ball and sob forever.

Everything in my world was upside down. But there were some simple facts.

First, I'd watched Lennox Lincoln-Ward masturbate . . . to me.

Secondly, I'd stolen information from him.

Third, Lennox proved in front of *everyone* that he had a thing for me.

And finally, I'd come with Rhys to the gala event. And then, I'd made out with aforementioned Lennox, nearly banging him in the gardens and then riding him in the scullery like a seasoned seductress.

Who the hell was I? None of this was my life. I was hardly a femme fatale.

But tonight you are.

The worst part of this whole damn thing was a part of me liked him. Or at the very least, was drawn to him. I couldn't fight the attraction. There was no more walking around pretending that I didn't orient myself around him, even if it was for express avoidance. Even if I could tell myself that I was around him for my own protection, so I could watch him better. It was a lie. I *wanted* to be around him.

I *wanted* his attention. I'd been pulled to Lennox like a magnet since the first moment we met.

I could still feel his lips on mine. The way his tongue delved into my mouth. His hands on my body. His lips on the tips of my breasts. The low growl he'd made as he'd pushed inside me still reverberated in my ears, making my body and skin hum with awareness, and arousal, and adrenaline.

I wanted Lennox Lincoln-Ward.

For once in my life, I felt like I was important to someone. I'd felt beautiful. Like someone saw me. The *real* me. Someone thought I was beautiful and stunning. Someone thought I mattered.

Yes, we'd been interrupted, but then there had been a deeper shift. As we'd worked to take care of Aurora, there had been this connection between us. As if we could actually like each other. Like we could speak and get along. Maybe we were just at the tipping point where hate and distress turned into something else. And then, that sweet, sweet friction as I'd worked my slick heat over him, making him come . . . all over the both of us.

Then I'd said the wrong thing. And there had been the disgust in his eyes, the hatred in his voice, the anger on his cruelly beautiful face.

Because your father told you that's what you should think of me?

I'd wanted to bite back at him, to yell, to seethe. I hated that Lennox's fascination with me began and ended with my father. I hated that the moment he was wounded, he assumed it was my father doing the wounding through me.

My father had nothing to do with me!

Your father has everything to do with you. Your father arrested his.

Your father asked you to spy on him.

And Lennox still doesn't know.

I winced just thinking about it, because I *had* done what my father asked. Not necessarily blindly, but I had done what I was told to do. And I hadn't asked any questions. I hadn't wondered if maybe I shouldn't have been doing it. Or why it felt icky. I'd done it. But now, as Lennox's words rang in my head, I couldn't help but wonder what piece I wasn't seeing, because there had to be more to the story. Yes, my father had lied about his involvement, but even knowing that now . . . there *had* to be more than my father simply investigating Lennox's.

Investigated is a kind word, Sloane. A very kind word.

I was used to seeing the pieces and making them fit the puzzle. And all puzzles eventually made sense. You just had to find out where your thread was, how to pull it correctly, and I still couldn't quite figure it out.

When we got back to Pembroke, it was late enough that the lights in the dining hall were on as the cooks began to work on the Sunday morning pastries. Sera stumbled sleepily into the en suite and started a shower I knew would last until dawn, and I got a single text message from Keaton—not Lennox notably—that Aurora was spending the night at the Huntington mansion with everyone else and would be back at the dorms tomorrow. Keaton promised to keep Phin away from her, and as pissed as I was at Lennox, I trusted him and Keaton to protect Aurora. Lennox obviously cared for her deeply, maybe more than he even cared for himself.

I zipped out of my dress, relieved to be able to breathe in a full gulp of air for the first time in several hours. But after I scrubbed my face clean, peeled off the lashes that Sera had made me wear and scooped my hair back into my usual tiny little ponytail, I stared at myself in the mirror. The same green eyes, fair skin, and completely unremarkable face stared back at me.

It was as if that hidden fairy princess that I had felt like tonight hadn't existed. Without the adornments and without the gaze of the fairy prince, I was just plain old Sloane again.

I checked the clock. It was close to five. Which meant my father would be awake, getting ready for his morning run while he glanced through any new APBs that came out while he was asleep. I picked up the phone and made a call, even though I wasn't entirely sure what I was going to ask for.

"Sweetheart?"

"Hey, Dad."

"Sloane, the sun hasn't even risen, what are you doing up?"

I fidgeted with the hem of my t-shirt. Part of my Sloane uniform was a t-shirt and boy shorts to bed. Hair pulled back. Nothing sexy or beautiful. "I have a question. And I need you to be honest with me."

"Sure. I'm always honest with you."

A brief shot of anger hit my blood, followed by hurt. How quickly he seemed to forget that he'd lied to me. He'd lied to me and while he hadn't known that Lennox was torturing me, he'd inadvertently made everything worse by not giving me all the facts.

"The Lincoln-Ward case . . ." I started, and then paused, not knowing how to phrase the question I wanted to ask.

There was a moment of silence, and then a long sigh. "Sloane, is this what you really want to talk about? It was a complicated case. I worked on it. That's all."

"Yes, it's what I want to talk about!" The hiss

of Sera's shower through the en suite door mimicked the blood rushing through my ears. "You asked me to pull information on Lennox—don't you think I deserve to know why? Don't you think I deserve some context? Some background?"

I knew he'd agree. I had a point. If he could ask me to spy on Lennox, then he could tell me what I needed to know.

"All right," Dad said, sounding suddenly very tired. "What do you want to know?"

"Just—more. I guess. More than what you've told me."

A heavy exhale. "It's not a pleasant story."

"I know it's not," I replied. "Ponzi scheme stories rarely are."

"I meant it's not a very pleasant story about *me*," Dad clarified. "I meant what I said to you last week. I'm not—I'm not proud of this chapter in my life. I just want you to know that before I begin."

I didn't know what to say to that.

Investigated is a kind word.

What had my father done?

"So their father, Boris Lincoln-Ward," Dad started.

"Billionaire Ponzi scheme guy."

"Exactly. When he got caught, he was quick to argue the charges until we leveraged him for someone even bigger. He was part of a Ponzi scheme, as you know, but he was also connected to a woman who had thwarted Europol for nearly a decade. She not only swindled rich men out of their money, but the people they worked for, and companies as well. Up until Boris, she had walked away with over ten million dollars. She used different aliases and was hard to track. When we caught Boris, he was already going to go to jail for a long time. Word was that he had hidden billions of his own money away, and not all of it was recovered. But he was willing to work with us on a deal. Less time. He was only going to do fifteen years, instead of the thirty many of the complainants called for. His children's trusts weren't to be touched. In exchange, he gave us the woman."

"Okay," I said, still not seeing why this would have been worse than any other criminal investigation. "So he traded away an associate?"

"Her name was Graciella de Marco," Dad said. "She's basically an international thief. As best we can imagine, but with access to the kind of people and money most of us only dream about. Her mother was a minor heiress of a Greek shipping tycoon who made bad investments, lost all his money. Her family was destitute. Not much was known about her after her family had lost everything. Either way, she wanted to go back to living a bountiful life, thus the criminal escapades. She'd been on the scene for a decade. Finding rich men, not just getting them to fall in love with her and allowing her to live the lavish lifestyle, but to invest in things that she suggested. Invest in her 'friends', invest in businesses she would talk up to them. Businesses that didn't actually exist. Before we caught her, she was able to take off with a lot of money. Most of it American. She was the bureau's white whale for over a decade. So when Boris offered to give her up—well. It was two birds with one stone, in a way. Except . . ."

He trailed off, clearly hesitant to say what he needed to say next.

"Except?" I prompted.

"You have to understand, once I had my teeth in Boris, I wasn't about to let him go. I was tenacious, and it took two years of my life to pin him down and nail him for what he was doing. Men like him are slippery—so slippery—and they rely on charm and camouflage to get by, and it was the same with Graciella. After years of watching the both of them slip through the net time and time again, I had to make sure. I had to make sure that everyone would know their names. I had to make sure not only that they were caught, but that if they got away, the world would still know every terrible, criminal thing they did. So instead of bringing them in quietly, like we'd arranged with Boris, I arranged for something more . . . visible."

"Visible?"

"Graciella wasn't just an associate of Boris's, she was his mistress. He thought he'd have one last liaison with her before he betrayed her to us, and that's when I arrested them. I tipped off the press as well, so that it was as much of a spectacle as I could make it. And it worked—both Boris and Graciella had their sins aired out for the world to see. If they ever get out of prison, there will be no more victims left for them, no more slipping away into the shadows."

"Dad, that's not visible. That's *lurid*."

A heavy noise of agreement. "I hadn't factored in the human cost, I suppose. With Boris's wife being a princess, it attracted for more, um, intense speculation than I could have foreseen. It embarrassed Lennox's mother, the entire royal family, and dragged their good name through the mud. It must have been quite devastating for the children."

I thought back to that letter I'd found. The one that talked about *Vater*.

None of this still explained who Nicholas was or why Lennox had been writing to him.

But it did explain something else.

"So this is why Lennox hates you," I said in a dull voice. *This is why Lennox hates me because of you.* "Not merely the arrest, but the humiliation you caused doing it."

My father sighed. "I recognize that his children probably see me like a monster. I was the one who encouraged Boris to make the deal because I wanted de Marco too. I arranged the public arrest, and I embarrassed their mother. Embarrassed *them*."

Embarrassed them.

I got it now. I understood why it was more than his dad being a criminal and my dad being a cop.

It was because of my father that their mother was humiliated. That everyone in the world—including an eighth-grade Sloane—knew what their father had done and whom he'd been fucking while he did it.

With my mother gone, and Dad working ninety-nine percent of the time, it was sometimes easier for me to stay for summer sessions at boarding school, but I remembered seeing the coverage even in my school dorm. It had dominated the news media for months. It was sordid.

People had lost their entire life savings. And maybe the investors could be written off as greedy, but what made it worse was that their workers, their staff, all the innocent people around them . . . they'd lost everything too. And to cause that much pain while you were gallivanting around the Med with a gorgeous woman who wasn't your delicate, princess wife . . .

No wonder the media ate it up.

No wonder Lennox was so scarred by it.

Why did you think I was greedy? Because of my father?

"So you had me looking into Lennox because what, you think he's doing the same thing his dad did?"

"No, nothing like that. But there are suspicious deposits and withdrawals in his accounts. And we couldn't touch his trust because the grandparents are the trustees. Their parents, of course, have put money into it, but their trusts were off limits. All we can do is monitor their banking activity. It's always been my theory that

Lincoln-Ward wasn't entirely honest. All his money isn't gone. My guess is he's squirreled some away. Once he serves the reduced sentence of fifteen years, he would need something to come back and live on. I theorized that he's found a way to access it and that it's going through his son's trust to launder it. Make it clean money so when he gets out of jail, Lennox can give him the cash. Then he can start over."

My stomach roiled. "Dad, I'm not sure—"

"Look," he interrupted me. "I know he's your classmate, possibly your friend, but it's entirely plausible. I mean, you *know* it's possible. You're too smart not to see that. That's why you agreed to investigate."

Jesus Christ. I *had* agreed to investigate. But I still hadn't given Dad everything. And I didn't know how to walk that back now because Lennox was right. I had believed exactly what my father told me. Without any question. I was just like him.

But worst of all, any hope that I would once again be that fairy princess I was the night of the gala—or be seen as beautiful by anyone—died. That dream turned to ash in my palms.

Because now that I understood . . . now that I knew why Lennox hated my father, why Lennox was so angry . . . I knew there was no way we could ever be together.

Because beyond anything else, Lennox Lincoln-Ward was proud. Haughty.

An arrest he could have eventually forgiven—but a public disgrace? Deep and visible shame?

He could never forget that, never forgive it. And if he found out that I'd been looking through his things, helping my father ensure his could never, ever reclaim any scrap of wealth or dignity . . .

I shivered with misery.

If he found out . . . it would be all over then.

CHAPTER FOURTEEN

LENNOX

I RETURNED TO campus the next morning with a hungover Aurora. After I settled her in her room, I made sure she drank enough water and took enough aspirin for her to feel better after a long nap, and then I went back to my room. I'd just toed off my Oxfords when a big fist pounded on my door.

"It's unlocked, you pillock," I yelled as it swung open to reveal the broad shoulders of Keaton Constantine.

"I know you didn't forget about the Hellfire meeting tonight," he said, as I threw myself back on my bed with a groan.

I covered my face with a pillow. "Fuck."

"Yeah," he said in sympathy.

"They want us in dinner dress?"

"You know they do."

I swore again, dropping the pillow to the side and blinking up at my ceiling. I was wrecked from last night. I felt like I was walking through a knee-high marsh, every step exhausting and bitter.

My brain was still whirling, and it refused to give me peace.

"Fine," I mumbled. "I'll get ready."

Keaton made a noise of assent, like he'd had no doubt all along, and then he left to go get ready himself.

THE HELLFIRE CLUB was founded in 1871 to do what most clubs back then were meant to do—forge alliances and consolidate power. The first Hellfire Club members at Pembroke were the sons of robber barons and senators, and through the friendships they forged at school, and through the equally connected peers they invited in, they went on to find their own wealth and power too. And so on and so forth, each previous generation of Hellfire members nurturing the next—opening doors, making introductions—until *that* generation could help too. It was a web of green paper and cigar smoke stretching back a century and a half, and it was an invitation that would have been foolish to refuse.

Yes, I was a prince, but my father was also a disgraced, imprisoned billionaire. I didn't have the luxury of rejecting a foothold like this, even if it came tied with incredibly annoying strings. Like the occasional dinner in the city. Like being examined by Hellfire alumni like we were livestock at a meat market.

And while it was undoubtedly annoying, I'd grown up around this kind of secretive, self-important pomp and circumstance. I knew how to play their game better than they did. It had been invented by my forefathers, after all.

The cars came for us at noon, and we ducked dutifully inside—Keaton hustling me into a car with him and Owen before I could get within fifteen feet of Phineas.

Or *fucking* Rhys.

November wind buffeted us in our tuxedos and dress coats before we could escape into the warmth of the car. I welcomed the wintry chill. The cold reminded me that I was still alive, even though I felt like I was dead inside.

What the hell was wrong with me?

You know what's wrong with you.

Sloane. Fucking Sloane.

I flung myself back into the leather seat and closed my eyes before Keaton and Owen could try to talk to me. I was in no mood for chitchat, not after last night. Not after all the ways the night had gone all fucked up.

First, Rhys had had his goddamn hands all over Sloane.

Second of all, she looked like she was into it.

Third of all, she'd looked like something out of an ethereal dream, all that vibrant blue-green gossamer. The bodice of her dress, the deep vee. Her lips stained pink, and plump, and glistening, and so god damn soft. And why for fuck's sake had she tasted so good?

Her eyes, everything about her had been amplified. Enhanced. She looked like a fairy. All of her sparkled. All of her shimmered. All of her shined. And despite her slender frame, that dress had shoved her tits under her chin somehow, giving her enough cleavage to make my stupid mouth water.

And then all I could think about was Rhys putting his hands on her. And I'd snapped.

Way to go, Neanderthal.

I had literally picked her up over my shoulder and dragged her out of there.

Let's not forget the crazy shit in the garden.

Motherfucker. I'd been about to stick my dick inside her. Okay technically *had* stuck my dick inside her . . . just the tip though. That didn't count, did it? I couldn't lie. That's where we'd been going. We'd been about to shag in the garden. I could still feel her sweet tightness around the tip of my dick.

Just the tip, motherfucker. Like a moron.

I knew better. Hell, I'd never had sex without a condom. *Ever.* I wasn't that dumb. There were a few lessons my mother had imparted quite well on me. Like don't knock anyone up. Don't be an idiot. Do not leave illegitimate children to be accounted for later.

But still, with Sloane, I was ready and more than damn willing to slide home . . . bare. To feel her heat, to have her velvet slickness mold around me and make me her bitch.

I'd been riding on the edge of dangerous arousal. But then Aurora had come in. Drunk and sobbing and distraught. How in the world had I been able to pull back?

You were a saint, that's what it is.

But then everything had changed, and I had fucking relearned who Sloane really was. My destruction . . . wrapped in a tight-arsed package that was difficult to ignore. She was so casual about it all when her father had *ruined* my family's life.

I'm some sort of revenge plan?

She'd been angry, furious, pushing and shoving me until somehow we ended up on those soft cushions with me between her legs.

I'd have to hurt you for a thousand years to make up for all the things you've done to me, she'd hissed—but what about me? What about all the things her family had done to me?

How can you even want her?

Well, that was a problem with my cock. Motherfucker didn't listen. It was all his fault.

Even as I tried to nap my way down to Manhattan, the damn thing twitched in my pants. He was thinking about how soft she was. How damn near perfect she felt. My brain conjured up that feeling of her slick wet heat and sent a buzz up my spine that nearly snapped my head clean off. Right from the base of my spine straight to the top of my neck. It was such a jolt that I thought I was going to die. And die in heaven, no less.

But then that high had all come crashing down.

Goddamn Sloane.

The drive ended up being uneventful and boring. Owen tapped through emails on his iPad—his family ran Montgomery Media, a group focused mostly on magazines and apps, and his parents treated him like a baby COO—and Keaton watched rugby footage on his phone with a scowl on his all-American face. I was grateful for the silence though, because I couldn't handle all the feelings vibrating up my spine, and I was terrified that if I opened my mouth to make polite conversation, something ugly and vulnerable would come tumbling out.

Like my fury at Rhys. My extra fury at Phin for making Aurora cry.

My fury at Sloane.

My hunger for Sloane.

The strange dagger of pain between my ribs whenever I thought of the look Sloane gave me last night before she left. As if *I'd* been the arsehole.

Had I been?

My mind circled back to Phin and how much I'd like to smash his teeth in for hurting my twin. Yes, that was a safe anger, a safe feeling. Much safer than thinking about Sloane.

I let the anger fill me all through the drive there, pooling in my gut like oil ready to burn. I'd find Phin at the dinner and then throw him out the window, right onto Fifth goddamn Avenue.

"Thank fuck," Keaton groaned, stretching his giant body as the car rolled to a stop in front of a narrow but ornately trimmed mansion squashed between two equally ornate apartment buildings. Gas lamps flickered on sconces outside the wide, old door, and the huge windows glowed with the kind of light that only came from rooms paneled in wood and upholstered in leather and velvet. A stone lion guarded either side of the stairs leading up to the black-lacquered door, their claws anchored in flames and their mouths parted in toothy snarls.

It looked every inch a nineteenth century industrialist's house, opulence built on the backs of the poor, and for over one hundred years, it had been a den of old money and even older sins.

Hellfire House.

Keaton got out first, and Owen followed, not looking up from his iPad as he did. Owen had grown up among the moneyed bustle of Manhattan, and so he was as unimpressed by Gilded Age mansions as I was by castles back home.

Keaton himself only gave the building a brief, appraising glance. I knew he was only a member because it was expected of him and not because he wanted to follow in his brother Winston's footsteps and become a captain of industry or whatever it was Winston Constantine did with his time. In fact, I'd bet my family's private Austrian ski chalet that the moment Keaton graduated from Pembroke, he'd be gone from this world altogether. Off playing rugby and fucking his girlfriend. Not clinking port glasses and comparing big game hunting trips.

We were greeted at the door by staff who took our coats and escorted us to the drawing room, where a large fire crackled in a stone fireplace and servers circulated with aperitifs. A few older Hellfire alumni were in here, but most were still cloistered somewhere else, probably attempting to seal a few more corrupt deals before dinner officially began.

Keaton turned to face me as we were walking inside. "Don't do anything stupid tonight. Even my Constantine hands might be tied if you attack a Yates."

"I'll do whatever the fuck I want," I muttered.

"Whatever happened with Aurora last summer broke him, man."

"So that gives him the right to make her cry?" I demanded, but I didn't waste any more breath on Keaton, because we were in the room now and I could see *him*.

Phin.

Fucking Phin, just sitting by the fireplace with a lazy smile and his hair all over the place. Drink in fucking hand, like he didn't have a care in the world aside from drinking and finding his next lay.

"You fucking wanker," I seethed, striding over to him and yanking him to his feet by the lapels of his tuxedo jacket. I was aware of the interested stares of the other men in the room, and just as aware when they went back to their conversations, as if used to pre-dinner drinks erupting into violence. "I should kill you right now for what you did to my sister."

Phin's smile faded, but he didn't shove me off him, he didn't try to wrestle free. He only glared at me over the collar of his jacket. "You know, no one ever asks what Aurora did to *me*," he said. "And I'll have you know that last night, she was the one to stop things between us. *She* was the one to walk away, not me. Yes, I found someone else after, but only because she made it clear she was done with me."

"I don't believe you," I said.

"Well, believe this—do you really think Aurora would have let me live if I'd promised her something and then ended up inside someone else?"

I loosened my grip.

"She walked away first," Phin continued. "If

she hadn't, she would have shoved me into a meat grinder, and you know it."

I let go of his tuxedo. He was right. Aurora had been devastated last night, but if Phineas had *truly* screwed her over, she would have killed him first. *Then* cried about it.

"And it's not my fault I had to take care of the blue balls your sister gave me," Phin muttered, and I grabbed his lapels again.

"If you talk about my sister one more time, I will throw you into this fire and not think twice. I fucking mean it."

"Boys," Owen said in a bored, cold tone, coming up to us and leaning against the side of the fireplace. "Can we not with the murdering before dinner? I haven't eaten yet, and bailing one of you out of jail is certain to put me off my appetite."

I let go. Reluctantly.

Rhys sauntered over to our little scene, clapping slowly. As if Phin and I had just put on a show for him.

I leveled a look at him. "You don't want to start with me, Rhys. Not after the shit you pulled this weekend."

"Oh, is that right? It was nice to see you finally get off your ass, by the way."

I blinked at him. "If you know what's good for you, mate, you'll shut it."

Rhys chuckled. "No need to get touchy with me. I did you a goddamn favor."

I scowled at him. "What the hell do you mean?"

"Well, I knew you weren't ever going to fucking do anything about Sloane unless you were pushed. And now I've pushed you. You're welcome."

I glowered at him, taking a step in his direction. But Owen was quick and inserted himself between us. "Not worth it. Dinner, remember?"

Phineas's chuckle was low, as if he lived to see what was going to go down. He also probably wouldn't mind seeing my face beaten and bloodied after I just threatened to hurl him into the fire. Tosser.

Keaton merely rolled his eyes. "You two have done this already. Let it go."

I glared at our de facto leader. "You hear that bullshit he's spewing?"

"Rhys, you're a dick," Keaton said in the beleaguered tone of a parent with squabbling children. "We love you, dude, but seriously, stop being a gaping dickhole." Keaton looked at me and threw his hands up to say, "Satisfied now?"

No, I was not goddamn satisfied.

Rhys shrugged. "She's no longer of interest to me anyway."

Say what? He'd put me through the wringer and now he was bored? "What the fuck do you mean? You did all of this just to tick me off?"

Rhys gave me a level stare, and a chill ran through my body because it was as if, for once, the shield that he used as a barrier to ever having to feel any emotion came down for just one moment, and his eyes were clear. "You wanted her. You acted like you didn't, but you did. It was apparent to everyone here. And hopefully, it's apparent to you now. You were never going to take any step besides just torturing her, which I'm a fan of. But it was boring. I wanted to see if I could make you do something. And you did. Congratulations."

I swiped Owen's hand off my chest. "Relax, I'm not going to hit him."

Owen's smirk was cold. "So you say. But your emotions are running rampant. Lock them down. We're Hellfire. We're all mates here."

I growled at him. "Some mate."

Rhys grinned at me. "You know, I can always go and kiss her again."

I started toward him, and this time Keaton

stepped in front of me then shook his head. "That's enough."

"Fine." But then, I dug deep for the one thing I knew would rattle Rhys. "You know what? It's not really going to work out with Sloane. Irreconcilable differences. Instead of her, you know who is well fit for me? Serafina. I danced with her last night. I'm pretty sure you saw."

Just like that, the walls went right back up around Rhys, and he lifted a brow. He didn't say anything, so I pushed further. "God, that arse. You haven't lived until you've palmed that perfect piece of an arse. She's so slender but has curves just where they matter. A simple squeeze could take you to heaven." I gave Rhys an evil grin, and I could see his lip curl as he scowled at me.

"Stay the fuck away from Serafina."

I laughed then. "Why should I? She is very interested in me."

Rhys started towards me, but Keaton stood in front of him. Thanks to rugby, Keaton was massive. Even Rhys didn't want that kind of fight. "I warned you because we're friends. You put your hands on Serafina, I will end you."

Keaton rolled his eyes. "You two are ridiculous. Rhys, you might be the worst."

"The thing with Serafina and me, it's private."

Keaton shrugged. "Yeah, well, you're both dicks." He turned to me. "Better figure out your shit with Sloane."

I rolled my shoulders. "Like I said, irreconcilable differences."

Rhys threw up his hands. "Jesus Christ, for a fucking smart guy, you're an idiot. Whatever issues you've got with her, she's under your skin. There's no way you're letting her go."

Owen clapped me on my shoulder. "He has a point. You've been obsessed with Sloane since she got here. I don't understand it. Is she worth this messy shit? Is any girl? Whatever irreconcilable difference this is, maybe you should find a way to reconcile that because we have all seen it. You literally carried her out of there over your shoulder. I hate to agree with him, but Rhys is right."

Rhys settled into a chair and leaned back into it. "I'm always right. Just none of you are smart enough to agree with me."

I watched my friends. They had a point. Sloane was like a promise, a pact, a vow, signed with our blood. She was mine to torment. Or maybe I had it wrong. She was my tormentor. I couldn't shake my feelings for her off no matter how hard I tried. And I needed to figure out just what I was going to do about it. My dick chimed in with a, 'Oh, she's mine. If you can't get her for me, I'll be taking the reins.'

Sloane was in my blood. There was no purging her from my system. I hated that Rhys was right. He was just so goddamn smug about it all. I had nearly kicked him in the arse. Sloane is the key, though, to sorting myself out.

But would we even be able to get past everything? Was that even a possibility for us?

The real question is, can you get over what her father did to yours?

The question dogged me through dinner and through the interminable drinks after. Ostensibly tonight's meeting was so we could discuss nominations—each year's outgoing seniors nominated freshmen to replace them in the club—but it was a farce, and we all knew it. The incoming Hellfire members had already been decided years ago. Probably at fucking birth.

If you had a house in Bishop's Landing or an uncle or a godfather who'd been in the club, then you were in. Letting the current members pretend to choose was the most token of gestures.

So I tuned out the nomination talk, and the inevitable turn of the conversation toward the initiation ceremony that would happen at the end of the year, and I thought of Sloane. Of her hateful father, of the dark months that followed my father's arrest when paps crowded outside our house trying to catch glimpses of Boris's betrayed wife.

When even after our retreat to Liechtenstein, the internet teemed with the worst kind of rumors and gossip, and my mother used to cry alone in the dark of the library, hoping no one would notice.

But inevitably my traitorous mind drifted back to Sloane herself. To her full mouth and perceptive, green gaze. To the watchful, careful way she held herself, like a knife waiting patiently inside its sheath.

To the way her mouth parted in something almost like wonder when she came.

To the way she *smiled* when she came.

For the first time in four years, I had no idea what I wanted. And it terrified the shit out of me.

CHAPTER FIFTEEN

SLOANE

SERAFINA FOUND ME curled up in a ball on my bed when she came in from brushing her teeth. She'd slept in until the November day was bright and silver outside our window, but I'd barely slept at all, kicking off my blankets and tossing all over and generally just being miserable. And now it was nighttime again and I'd done nothing with my day except brood and sulk like a goddamned girl. I mean, I *was* a goddamned girl, but still. I hated it.

I couldn't stop seeing Lennox's face in the scullery shadows from the night before.

Why did you think I was selfish? Greedy?

Get the fuck off me.

"Oh my god, do your feet hurt as much as mine do? I don't care how pretty those Jimmy Choo's were, they were *not* worth it. Also, I was talking to Nika Monroe from Croft Wells, I guess some girl got attacked at a party two nights ago, but she managed to fight the guy off. Scary as hell, right? Can you imagine if something like that happened here—" She cut herself off as her gaze slid over me.

"Hey." She approached the bed and eased herself onto it, tucking her feet under her body and settling in next to me. "What's the matter?"

"I don't know," I whispered.

She laughed. "Um, I highly doubt that you don't know what's going on."

"Well, as it turns out it's not really going to work with Lennox."

Concern etched itself onto her face. "What are you talking about? The way he picked you up and tossed you over his shoulder, god that was so hot. Tell me why it's not going to work. That's ridiculous."

I shook my head. "It's just not."

Sera rolled her eyes. "Whoever this is, are you done whining yet? Bring Sloane back. My badass friend who thinks anything can be done with a switch blade and some hot glue."

I did love my switch blade, and hot glue could fix anything but—not this.

"I'm not in the mood, Sera."

She frowned and patted my knee. "What in the world is going on?"

"I realized that everything I'm doing is futile."

Sera grabbed hold of my knee and rubbed. "All right, spill it. Tell me everything. And if we're going to go kill someone, at least let me change into something chic but comfy. I don't want to get blood on my favorite bathrobe."

I laughed and then broke into a sob.

Her eyes went wide. "Hey, now you're really freaking me out. What's going on?"

God it was so weak, but I couldn't help the sob. "It's just never going to happen. And I just, I don't know why, but it hurts. It was so much better when I didn't let myself feel anything."

"Lennox is an idiot, Sloane. He's clearly all about you. He was willing to fight Rhys to have you. And let's be clear, he's the lucky one."

"Well, doesn't matter," I said around a sniffle. "He doesn't see it that way now."

She blinked slowly once, then twice. "I'm going to kill him."

"It's not even his fault. He has a right to be mad, sort of. Okay, so after he picked me up like the stupid caveman that he is, everything was going great. We were in the maze, he was kissing me, and it was amazing, and I've never felt like it before. Just beautiful and sexy, and just . . . hell, it was . . . incredible."

Sera was quiet, and she just kept patting my knee as we talked. So, I walked her through everything. How much I wanted him. How much I'd been willing to give him. And how close I had come to giving it to him. Then Aurora, and then his subsequent blow up, which ended with the conversation with my father. The revelation of what he'd really done to the Lincoln-Wards all those years ago.

When I was done, Sera stared at me. "Jesus Christ. When you go big, you go *big*. Also, let's call my concierge doctor and get you on the pill. I don't care how hot all that 'I want to fuck you bare' shit is. There's no need to be careless." She paused. "It is really hot though."

"I don't even know what I was thinking," I mumbled. "It just felt so good, and I could smell him, and he smelled like metal and flowers, and I couldn't even breathe for how much I wanted him to do it. You know?"

"I'm not sure I do," Sera said softly, but there was a line between her brows as she looked away from me to the floor. As if she was thinking about someone else, someone who wasn't here right now.

I had an idea of who it might be. "And let's be clear, so that there's no confusion with us," I added. "You and I both know Rhys was only kissing me to make you jealous."

Sera shuddered, looking back to me with a face that was all pretty haughtiness once again. "First of all, we're not talking about Rhys. Second of all, *hardly.* Third of all, the only Hellfire Club idiot I care about right now is Lennox and what he's done to you."

"But you see, it's not even his fault. I'm not only revenge, Sera, I'm *deserved* revenge. He's right to want that revenge, he's utterly right to hate my family for what we've done to his. If I were in his shoes, I might have already killed him by now."

Sera lifted a brow. "You are kind of prone to murder though."

No lies detected.

"Right? I wouldn't ask any questions, so how can I expect him to ask questions? How could I expect him to give me the benefit of the doubt?"

She nodded sagely. "Well, honey, the thing is, do you like him?"

I wiped my nose with the back of my hand, only mildly grossed out when snot came back and met me. "I didn't think I did. But then he was kissing me and it just—god, it felt good. And much different than when Rhys kissed me."

"What did you feel when Rhys kissed you?"

I shrugged. "I don't know. Like, it was nice. Even fun, I guess. But I don't know. When Lennox kisses me, it's like I've been lit on fire on the inside, you know?"

Sera grinned at me. "You like him. That's good. I'm surprised I have to be the one to tell you this, but direct is always better. No dancing around. You've done that enough. Has it worked for you?"

I frowned at that.

"Yeah, so maybe you don't do that anymore. Maybe you should open up with him. If this was me, you would be telling me to just deal with it. No pussy-footing around, not be afraid of it, just deal."

I leveled my gaze on her. "So is this the time we talk about Rhys or not?"

Serafina wrinkled her nose and then pursed her lips as if she'd smelled something gross.

"I told you, we are *not* talking about him. Besides, could you imagine addressing anything with him head on? He's impossible to talk to. Ever tried having a conversation with a flat-out dick?"

I nodded sagely. "I still have a point." Because while Rhys deigned to toy with me, I had known I was only a mere substitute for Sera. The two of them had been in the same boarding schools since the lower grades. I couldn't explain it, but they had this *thing*. "Fine, I appreciate your advice, but Lennox is not going to listen to me."

"Maybe he will. You won't know unless you try. And my friend Sloane isn't a coward. My friend Sloane deals with things no matter what may come."

I gave her a weak smile. "Thank you."

"Anytime. You are my rock. If I see you distressed over a guy, then I know you must really like him. Even if you can't get through to him, that's okay. Because you're awesome. And if he isn't going to see that, that's his loss. You're beautiful, and there's a sweet core in there. I don't know where it is, but it's in there."

I coughed a laugh. "Don't tell anyone."

"*Moi*? Never."

She pushed to her feet then. "Now, can you help me get the rest of this double-stick tape off from last night? The left side wouldn't come off in the shower, and now I'm regretting all my fashion choices."

I grinned up at her. "But you looked awesome

though."

"Thank you very much. Beauty before comfort, I always say."

She turned away from me, sliding her robe off to her waist. I started picking at the edge of the tape on her ribs, tutting at her whenever she flinched or fussed.

"Why don't you maybe go knock on Lennox's door?" she suggested as I got hold of the tape and peeled. "Aurora said they had one of their stupid Hellfire meetings in the city today, but I bet they're back by now."

I frowned. "Then I don't want to bother—"

Sera lifted a brow and pursed her lip, making me feel like I was a six-year-old who just spilled nail polish over her fancy dress. "Are you really going to make excuses?"

Was I?

Was I going to spend the rest of my life like I did today, tossing in bed and replaying every moment I spent with Lennox?

No. No fucking way.

And maybe this is the time to fix what you've done.

I thought of the letter in my safe right now, throbbing at the edge of my consciousness like Poe's telltale heart.

I sighed. "Actually, good point. Here." I'd gotten the tape to the edge of her breast, where she could reach it to pull off the rest. I definitely didn't want to be around when she had to pull it off certain sensitive parts of her skin; I wasn't sure my ears could handle the storm she was sure to swear up.

I grabbed my hoodie, and while she wandered into the en suite to see to the nipple-tape situation, I quietly opened my safe and pulled out the letter, tucking it into my hoodie pocket.

"Have fun," Sera said, poking her head out from the bathroom. "Don't do anything I wouldn't do. I mean, there's not much I wouldn't do, so that gives you a lot to do."

I snorted a laugh. "I'm not going to do any-thing."

"If you say so."

I pushed out of the room and moved down the hall towards the common balcony. The way the upstairs dorms were set up was that at the end of each hall, there were staircases leading down and up. There was a door to a balcony that was common for both sides. Boys and girls. But to get from one side of the hall to the other, you had to go downstairs and then go up the other stairs on the other side. And the doors at the top of the stairs were closed as it was past 10 p.m., and you had to have the keypad code to enter.

This was to keep the boys and girls on opposite sides. It was changed daily and communicated to the dorm mother and father. But of course, I had my own code. It was called *Sloane can climb buildings like Jason Bourne.*

Next to the door to the balcony, there was a window. As I opened it, I quietly glanced around for anybody coming along, then eased myself out onto the sill which was only six inches wide. Luckily, the lip on the boys' side ran all the way around like a ledge coming up the sides of the building. It wasn't uncommon to see the boys sitting in their open windows, straddling their windowsills on the lip that went around. I eased along it as quickly as I dared. I knew the hedges below would catch my fall if I did misstep. But it would still be unpleasant. And I'd likely get several thorns up my ass.

When I reached Lennox's room, I peered inside before opening the window. The room was dark and quiet—maybe he hadn't come back from the city yet. Disappointment mingled with relief: it was better that he wasn't here, surely, so that I could put the letter back.

But I wanted to see him again. Even after our

fight, even knowing how he'd look at me, how he hated me for what my father had done . . .

I wanted to see him.

Stuffing the feeling down, I used my student ID to lift the window hook from its eye, and I eased into his room. I was certain he would have his security team with him in the city, but I was less certain that there wouldn't still be someone here in the dorm. And while they didn't have any cameras in his room—no one needed to see how often the prince jerked off, after all—they could still be patrolling the corridors. I kept myself quiet as I lowered myself to the floor.

The letter I'd stolen from him burned a hole in my pocket.

You're just going to put it back and then you're going to leave.

But when I tiptoed back over to his laptop and pulled the letter out of my pocket, a deep rumbly voice said from behind me. "What the fuck are you doing here?"

Alarm and lust blurred together, but at least my brain was one step ahead. I jammed the letter under the stack of papers before I whipped around. "Um, hi."

Lennox sat up groggily, clearly in the middle of a nap. He was shirtless. The silvery light coming through the window cast shadows of the ripples of muscles along his chest and his belly. Obviously, he was ripped. Hell, the night I caught him stroking himself, he had been shirtless. But I'd been far too preoccupied with what his hand had been doing.

"Um, sorry. I—I should . . ." I tried to think of a good explanation as to why I was there that didn't involve me obsessing about him all day *or* the pilfered letter. "I don't have your number, and I wanted to talk to you. And I'm sorry. I shouldn't have snuck in here. It's sort of a bad habit."

His brows popped. "You call sneaking into a guy's room a bad habit?"

His voice was still sleepy, but amused too. Like last night hadn't even happened.

I rolled my shoulders. "I'm sorry. I'll go."

"Wait."

I turned to him as I got to the window. "No, it's fine. I'll just go back to where I came from."

"Jesus Christ, Sloane. Stop. Where are you going?"

"I'm sorry. I just—I felt bad about what happened in the scullery, and I wanted to apologize. I didn't think you'd be asleep already."

"I'm not anymore. I had a strange dream."

I swallowed hard. "Oh, okay. Right. You had a dream. So, anyway, I'll be going."

His chuckle was slow, and the sound made my belly weak. I wanted to run but forced myself to be brave. "Um, sorry about last night. About the greedy thing. I didn't mean any of it."

He sighed. Then he frowned. "I think part of me knows you didn't mean it. I don't know why I was such a dick about it. I'm sorry."

My brows lifted. "You're apologizing to me?"

He nodded slowly. "Yeah, I think . . ." He scrubbed his fingertips through his sleep-tousled hair. "Everything about you, everything about how you make me feel, has been so tangled up and twisted inside me, and it fucks me up, Sloane. It fucks me right up. And then I was feeling a little vulnerable considering what we'd gotten up to in the garden."

I blinked at him. Did he just say he was vulnerable?

He tilted his head at me. "I wish I knew what you were thinking right now," he murmured. "Sometimes I feel so fucking transparent around you, and you're . . ."

"Not transparent at all?" I suggested, and he smiled a little.

"Right."

It was the way I'd been made—the way I'd thought I wanted to be. But right now it felt awful; it felt like there were walls between us that could never be torn down, that couldn't even be tunneled through. I could viscerally feel the presence of the letter I'd just hidden, viscerally *feel* my deception thrumming in the room.

Maybe it was a good thing I wasn't so transparent after all.

"I should go, Lennox."

"Do you have to get back?" he asked. "Or could you stay so we could talk?"

"You're not going to have, like, security burst in here and arrest me, are you?"

A smile—sharp and charming—tilted at his mouth. "They know when to leave me alone. They did when we were in the maze, didn't they? Now stay. Stay with me."

I meant to say no—but somehow I found myself nodding and heading for the chair at his desk. Maybe I could hide my feelings from him, but I couldn't from myself.

I wanted to stay. I wanted to stay with my beautiful bully for hours and hours and hours.

Lennox chuckled low before snatching his sheets back. I could not help but stare as he pushed to his full height. My gaze lingered at every single fine muscle in front of me. He was built lean. Like a swimmer. Nice broad shoulders, tapered waist into boxer briefs. And wow, that looked like one hell of an erection.

Not that you care, because you don't care about erections. You care about . . . what the hell do you care about again?

I couldn't remember. My synapses were fried by looking at him. He walked over and took my hand. Something burned in his golden eyes—a desperate hunger that matched the one burning inside me right now.

"Come on," he whispered. "We don't have to do anything. I could just hold you."

I parted my lips to tell him that even holding me was a bad idea, but he pre-empted me.

"Just for a minute," he said in a husky voice. "Let me feel you against me for just a minute."

Lust shook me hard. "Just for a minute?"

"Or longer, if you like," he said roughly. "Unless I scared you in the maze last night."

Scared? More like infected me with a miserable desire nothing could ever shake.

I shook my head. "No. I liked it. It felt good, and I felt wanted, and . . . I felt pretty."

He raised a hand to my face and tucked my hair behind my ears, a gesture both gentle and possessive at the same time. "Don't you know that you're always pretty?"

I tucked my head down. "No, I know what I look like. I'm not like—"

"Do you? I don't think you do. Or at least you don't see clearly."

"But—"

He inclined his head towards the bed. "Come on, Sloane. I'm cold and I know you are too."

He eased into the bed and backed all the way up into the wall, making plenty of room for me to climb in. Most of the beds in the dorms were twins, but his was a full one, because of course it was, because he was a fucking prince and he got whatever he wanted.

And he wanted me right now.

Need was lacing the blood in my veins, and my chest was a mess of tight, swirling feelings. It made me want to run away, how he made me feel, and protect my heart before he could hurt it. But I was also no chicken shit. I swallowed hard and then climbed in next to him.

I rolled onto my back, and he propped himself up on his elbow and watched me. "So, sneaking into a guy's room is a habit?"

"Only when duty calls."

"Ah. You mean your little detective inspector

business."

"It's not a business," I corrected, looking up into his painfully pretty face. "I help people who need it. That's it."

"As long as you're not crawling into anybody's bed but mine," he said, and there was a rough edge to his voice. *Jealousy.*

"Would you care if I did?"

"You know I would."

We looked at each other for a long moment, neither of us speaking, neither of us even breathing. It felt like we were poised on the knife's edge of something.

"What were you really doing in here?" he asked quietly.

I hesitated and then spoke the truth. Or part of it at least. "I wanted to see you. After last night . . . I wanted to apologize. It wasn't my intention to hurt you, and I know with what happened between our fathers that you might think . . ." I trailed off. I wasn't sure what I could say next that wouldn't make everything worse.

He closed his eyes. When he opened them again, the gold irises burned with too many emotions to name. "I don't want to talk about it," he said, the words curt.

I winced, but I nodded. I understood.

"Can I ask you something?"

"Yes."

"Do you really like Rhys?"

I laughed at the unexpected conversation. "No. I mean, sure he's good-looking and all that, but it just didn't feel—I don't know, real? I figured he was running some kind of weird Rhys experiment."

"But you let him kiss you."

"Yeah. I mean, it's not like I have a mile-long line of guys begging to try and go out with me. It was flattering. And once I realized it kind of annoyed you, I wanted to do it again."

His jaw unhinged. "What? Sloane. You played me."

I shrugged. "Well, I didn't really play you. I like seeing you being a little jealous."

He nodded. "Noted."

As we laid there on his bed, we talked . . . really talked, I wondered why I instinctively avoided him for so long.

But one touch of his fingers on my cheek, to my shoulders and my elbow, and my head swam. It was intoxicating. And I wanted more.

"Hey, Sloane?"

"Yes, Lennox."

"Can I kiss you?"

I knew it was dangerous because we were in his room, and there was no way Aurora was going to come bursting in this time. No way she could accidentally save me from giving this boy more of my heart like she did last night.

But still, I nodded. "Yes."

Chapter Sixteen

Lennox

I THOUGHT I was dreaming at first. I full-on thought I'd woken up and my dream had manifested into reality. But no, she was here. In my bed. And she was talking to me. Considering what I'd said to her earlier, I didn't expect that. But here she was, still willing to talk to me after I'd been a jackarse.

I can fix that.

I leaned forward. I just wanted to be close to her. In no way did I mean for the kiss to go further than that.

But she made this soft exhale as I kissed her. Just a gentle brush of the lips, and then my brain somehow lost the battle with my dick, so I couldn't exactly focus.

Instead of lying there stiffly with her hands clasped over her belly, her hands loosened. One rose up to my face, just as I cradled hers in my hands. And then I gently licked across the seam of her lips, and she gasped, letting me in.

I sort of lost rational thought after that. She smelled like honeysuckle and something a little minty fresh. I'd meant for it to just be a kiss. I'd meant it to be soft—a sort of apology.

Instead, she gasped, and made this soft little whimpering sound at the back of her throat and well, I got a little carried away.

It wasn't my fault. She was just so damn soft.

Her skin was like satin. And everything about her was a mystery.

If I was being honest, Sloane wasn't the first girl who'd ever crawled into my bed. But she was the only one I'd ever wanted to. She thought she wasn't beautiful, but that was so not true. To me, she was stunning. Those eyes, her mouth, even the secrets of her body. Ninety-nine point nine percent of the time, she dressed like wearing a skirt was something she had to be forced into doing, but it didn't matter what she wore, because everything on her looked like it was made to be worn by her. Like it was made to show off her sharp edges and subtle curves.

Another moan from Sloane, and my ricocheting thoughts refocused on her.

Before I knew what was happening, Sloane molded her body to mine. And her tongue met me stroke for stroke. It was her who deepened the kiss. And it was me who lost control. I couldn't help but fall. Fall so deep into the abyss that I never wanted to come back out again. My skin buzzed as my dick got hard. All I could think of was her. How she felt. How she smelled. Her strong voice when she spoke. The secret smile when I caught one. Those vibrant green eyes of hers, as they always regarded me with stark honesty. God, I could fall for her.

You already have, you prat. Welcome to the party.

When Sloane molded her body against mine, I knew the right thing was to stop this. Nothing was sorted between us. I was still reasonably certain that I could never forgive what her father had done to my family, and I was still reasonably certain that she could never forgive me for what I'd done to *her.*

But somehow that didn't affect my craving to make her mine. It didn't temper at all the hot, tormenting need I had for her.

I didn't mean to roll on top of her. It wasn't planned exactly. But then, when my hips were nestled between her thighs, and she'd widened her stance, making room for me, I groaned. The head of my dick peeked out of the top of my boxers, and Jesus Christ, I rocked my hips against her. Ever so slightly. Her hips lifted to meet mine, and I swallowed the moan on her tongue.

The tingling in my balls was like a loud clanging bell, jolting me awake, making me want to do the things I had sworn not to do only a few hours ago. At least, in here, I had condoms in my nightstand. But fuck, I already felt woozy. I knew exactly what she felt like around the head of my dick. I knew that she'd be soft, and hot, and satin. And God, she was so wet.

I rolled my hips again, and Sloane met me with each one. Sliding my hands up over her hips, I bracketed her narrow ribs and then slid my hands farther up. The gentle curve of her breasts fit my whole hand, and I stopped breathing. "Jesus Christ, Sloane."

"Lennox."

Her voice was husky, warm. Aroused. I wanted to keep her in this space forever. When my thumb rolled over her nipple, she groaned and her hips swiveled. Then it was my turn to groan. Fuck, I was hard. All I wanted to do was shove my fucking boxers down, pull down the ridiculous pajama pants that she had on and take us back to where we were the night before in the maze.

She wriggled out of them for me, and then her hoodie, so it was just her in boy shorts and a tank top with no bra. I could viscerally recall how it felt to have the tip of my dick coated in her juices; I wanted to be back there. The slide of my dick against her clit had me groaning, even with the fabric of our underthings between us.

Fuck, if I kept this up, I was going to come inside my boxers. Or worse, all over her . . . again. And she wasn't some hook up. This was not some random situation. This was Sloane. She'd been under my skin from the moment she showed up at the school. And I was tired of staying away from her. But if I wanted to keep her, I needed to take it slow.

"Oh my god, Lennox."

With a growl, I rolled to the side, bringing her with me, pressing our lips together again.

She pulled back and tore her lips from mine. "Is something wrong?"

I kissed her gently again. "No. Nothing is wrong." I stroked my other thumb over her cheek, even as my palm gave her breast a squeeze. "I want you more than I've ever wanted anything, but I'm trying to take it slow."

She frowned at that. "Did I ask you to take it

slow?"

I chuckled. "No, you did not. But for once in my life, I'm trying not to be a dick."

She lifted a brow then. "Wow, this is a hell of a time to start that."

I chuckled softly. "I know, right? Look at me, great in conscience and feelings, and all kinds of shit." I kissed her again. Long, and slow, and deep. With a whimper, she rocked her hips against my thigh, and I understood. She was keyed up too. She needed this just as much as I did.

With my thumb teasing over her nipple, she arched into my body. My other hand slid from her face, down the soft skin of her slender arms, over her hip. And then at the hem of her boy shorts, I paused. I made sure that she met my gaze. "Can I touch you?"

With short breathy pants, she nodded. "Yes."

"If there's something you don't like, tell me, okay?"

She nodded vehemently, and then I let my fingers dip under the elastic of her boy shorts. Her hips were slender. I could easily trace the V-line of her hipbone. She parted her legs for me, and my fingers slid over her bare lips before finding her wet core. I bit back the string of curses as I paused.

Sloane wriggled her hips and stared at me with wide eyes. "W-why are you stopping?"

I swallowed hard. *Holy fuck.*

I squeezed my eyes shut. She felt incredible. "I'm stopping because you feel really good."

I slid my fingers gently in and out and then back up to her lips to tease her clit.

She continued to bite her lip, and I wanted that pleasure, so I leaned forward and nipped her. "You're so soft. I could do this all day."

I slid one finger inside her, and then a second. I cupped my hand just a little bit so the heel of my palm would rub her clit. And then, I slid in and out, and in and out, my other hand still covering her breast, teasing her nipple, kissing her softly. She kept arching into me, wanting more. Begging for more from me.

My body was screaming. My dick was so hard it might explode. I honestly thought it would. Was that possible? I certainly didn't want to find out, but if I wanted her, I had to show that I could be more than just that guy that used to torture her. Her hand clutched my shoulder. "Lennox, oh my god, I—"

I knew what was happening. I used my thumb, slid it through her wetness, and then rubbed at her clit ever so gently as I dipped inside her, back and forth, back and forth. Then on a low moan I planted my lips on her, drinking in the sounds of her coming apart over my fingers. Convulse and tighten. Convulse and tighten.

Her hips undulated against my fingers, and her walls squeezed me tight.

Jesus Christ, Sloane Lauder's coming was a hell of a thing to watch. And I wanted to spend my life watching it again and again.

I eased my fingers from her and pulled her even closer to me. "You are so beautiful."

Her face went pink again, and she ducked her head as if she was going to deny it, but she said nothing. After a long moment, her frown returned.

"But what about you?"

"I will take care of me later. This is about you. And I want you to stay here for a little bit, if you want."

"I can't sleep here. Hellfire boys might be immune to dorm checks, but I'm not."

"I know. But can I just hold you for a minute?"

She nodded. And as I wrapped my arms around her, I knew that for as long as she was in my arms, I'd sleep well.

CHAPTER SEVENTEEN

SLOANE

THE THING ABOUT good intentions is they never quite go how you planned.

I'd meant to leave Lennox's room.

The problem was, once he wrapped himself around me and held me tight, and tucked me into his shoulder, I had fallen asleep. Like the dead. And then at some point in the middle of the night, I'd woken up to the hard erection poking me in the ass.

And there had been snuggling and nuzzling and more kissing, and more fingers. His mouth sucking at my nipples, and I'd come again. And that was some time around four. I had wanted to touch him. I had wanted to explore and play, but he wouldn't let me.

In the dark, he'd whispered to me how beautiful he thought I was, how badly he wanted me.

He'd whispered apologies for being such a dick, which I was entirely here for. He'd apologized with his kisses and his soft touches. And we'd fallen asleep . . . again.

So when the sun streaked in at six, I knew it was too late. There was no way to easily sneak out. When I jerked up in bed, he stirred, trying to drag me back to bed. His hand was already poised to slide back between my legs to its new home. "Lennox, we can't. I have to go."

He frowned and whispered groggily. "We have time, don't we?"

I lifted my head and stared at the clock. "It's 6:05."

He snapped to attention then, whipping around to glower at the clock. "Fuck. I didn't mean for you to stay all night."

"I know."

In a flurry of arms and muscles and a very sexy expanse of bare male chest, he helped me find, then put on my discarded clothes. When he grabbed my hoodie off the floor, helping me into it, he frowned. "Do we try and sneak you out the door?"

I shook my head. "The prefects do the checks at six-thirty. There might be some walking around already."

He cursed and glanced at the window. "There's no way I'm letting you go back out there."

"I have to. I can't go out the door."

"Well, what if you stay in here till seven?"

"What, and casually walk out? Everyone will know I spent the night in here."

He lifted a brow. "Does that matter?"

I tilted my chin up and met his gaze so he could see that I meant what I was saying. "No, not at all. I just don't want you to get in trouble. My record is clean, not a single mark. Yours however . . ." I let my voice trail off. He was a senior and a Hellfire Club member, so likely it wouldn't be too bad a punishment. But he'd had more than a few disciplinary marks. Mostly for drinking and insubordination towards prefects and teachers. A mark like this could get him suspended. Or worse, go on his transcripts for colleges.

He nodded slowly. "Well, I can't let you climb out the window."

"We have no choice, Lennox. It's how I came in yesterday. It's safe."

His brow only furrowed deeper. "It's dangerous."

What was wrong with him? "How do you

think I got in here yesterday?"

"Sloane," he pleaded.

"Lennox." I mimicked him.

"Why are you so damn stubborn?"

"Why are *you* so stubborn?" This was the only way, and he knew it, so why was he fighting me?

"Christ, you could fall."

"Trust me, this is far less dangerous than when I've done it before. At least I can see my feet on the ledge this time."

He massaged the bridge of his nose. "Please don't tell me that."

I frowned. Nobody worried about me. No one. Not ever. I wasn't sure how I felt about his worry. "Relax. If anyone sees me out there, they'll just assume it's just me being weird. Or at the very least, me trying to assassinate you. No one will ever think that I'm actually *sneaking* out of your room after spending the night with you. And I'm good at climbing and sneaking. Promise."

He swallowed hard, then licked his lips as his gaze fell to my mouth. "Actually, maybe we should change that."

I lifted my brows. "What? Which part?" Then I zipped my hoodie tight.

He cleared his throat, and a faint blush crept up his neck. "Yeah. Look, obviously we uh, like spending time with each other."

I grinned. "Obviously."

"So, I mean, I don't want to make a big deal or whatever, but shouldn't we just do it the conventional way? The hell I care if anyone knows you spent the night with me? Let the prefects dock me points. Fuck them. Besides, Keaton would fix it if they tried."

I blinked. He wanted this in the open. Where everyone could see.

He didn't know me well enough to know that not wanting to hide me was probably the number one way to my heart. "Okay," I said softly.

The furrow eased then. "Excellent. Meet me at the big tree at one."

I thought a moment. "After history?"

"Yes."

I gave him a slow nod.

A smile opened up his face. His eerie eyes glittered with pleasure. "I'll see you then."

I grinned. "Right. So I'm going to go now."

He nodded slowly. "Yeah, you should do that."

I laughed. "You should let me go, so I can go."

"Right. I'm going to let you go out there. Where it's dangerous, or I could kiss you and keep kissing you until it's 8:30 and all the prefects are already off to class. No one would notice."

He was tempting me. "Except, I have class at eight."

He groaned. "I want to kiss you more."

"I want you to kiss me more too. But I gotta go."

I stood on my tiptoes and tilted my head up. He was so much taller than me. I kissed his chin at first, and then he laughed and tilted his lips down towards mine. It was only when his tongue was in my mouth that I realized I probably had morning breath. Why was his so damn minty?

I pulled away. "Oh my god, my breath."

He laughed. "I might have cheated. I have one of those Listerine breath strip things."

"What, and you didn't offer me one?" I turn to the window.

"You could just walk out the door," Lennox said, his voice tight. "If we're going public anyway."

"I'm not risking running into the prefects," I informed him. "It may be all right for you, Mr. Hellfire, but I can't have disciplinary shit on my transcript before I'm accepted to Georgetown. Not to mention, your disciplinaries are so long, this one might actually affect you."

"Dammit, Sloane—"

I was already standing and finding my hand-holds. I could feel Lennox's gaze as I tiptoed over the ledge all the way to the balcony and hopped down.

Only then did I feel him breathe.

After hopping the ledge to go back to the girls' side, I turned back to him and gave him a saucy smile and then winked. He just rolled his eyes and shook his head. When I sauntered into my room, Sera was sitting on her bed, cross-legged, fully dressed for class and waiting for me. "Oh my god, you are so late."

"I'm not. I have plenty of time to shower and get ready for class."

"Yeah, I know you do. But that's not the point. You're so late for me, because I have a seven o'clock seminar, and I need to be able to hear all the juicy details first. Did you bone?"

My face flushed. Sera jumped up off her bed. "Oh my god, you did."

I shook my head. "No, no. But I mean, we did kiss and *stuff*."

Sera's eyes went round. "Oh my god, 'and stuff'? You need to tell me everything." She frowned as she studied her watch. "God, I hate you. I only have ten minutes to get down the stairs and then eat, and then run to the seminar. But when I get back this afternoon, you and me, we're doing a full deconstruction. Do you get me?"

I laughed. "Yeah, I get you."

I watched my best friend prance out of our room. I could only laugh. I had never in my life snuck in before. This is a whole new experience, and I loved every moment of it.

AT ONE O'CLOCK, my palms were sweating. I had no idea what any of this meant. Were we together now? All morning my stomach was tied in knots. I was barely able to eat. I'd seen him a few times in the hallways, and he would give me this wide grin whenever he saw me. A couple of times he winked. We had history together, right before the lunch hour, and he took his usual seat, which was far behind me in the back. I could feel his gaze on me the entire time.

When that final bell rang to free us, we walked through the doorway together. It was packed and crowded as we all were trying to hurry up and get out to our respective lunch meetings and study groups. His pinky found mine for the briefest hair of a second, and he leaned close. "I have something to do, so I can't have lunch with you. But I'll see you at one, yeah?"

My skin heated, and I flushed. I was convinced everybody could tell. I was convinced everybody must know. But everyone around us acted completely normal. As if Lennox hadn't just been holding my hand. Or that I hadn't just spent the entire night in his bed. This was crazy.

So, as I marched towards the big tree in the center of the campus, my stomach knotted even more. I'd had lunch with Serafina and Aurora, and Serafina had showed amazing levels of restraint in not forcing me to talk. I think she gathered that I didn't quite want to tell Aurora yet. Lennox was her brother. It was complicated, and I didn't really know what was happening. I knew that when we got back this afternoon though, I'd have to tell her everything.

There was a part of me that was worried none of this was real, and that I'd imagined it all. But there he was, sitting on a blanket, underneath the big tree, looking as if he owned the damned thing. He had on a rumpled blazer, hair looking perfectly windblown. It wasn't fair that he looked so good.

When I approached, he smiled and then stood up, deftly coming towards me. I was hyper aware of how everyone might see whatever we might do, but then he smiled. And I promptly stopped giving a rat's ass. "Hey."

He grinned at me. "Hey to you too. How was lunch?"

"Good. You know, just the girls."

He grinned. "Did Serafina grill you?"

I shook my head. "Nope. I didn't really know what I could tell Aurora and what I couldn't."

He laughed. "You can tell Aurora. I told her first thing this morning."

"Wow, she didn't even say a word."

"Well, she was waiting for you to tell her."

I groaned. "Now she's wondering why I didn't tell her. Great. We should have coordinated."

He laughed. "She's my twin sister. Basically, as soon as the dorms were open to each side, she was knocking at my door wanting to know what the hell I'd been doing last night."

Heat suffused my skin. "Excellent."

"Look, I didn't go into detail. But I did tell her I was with you."

"Right. Okay." How was I going to navigate this?

"Relax, she was really happy."

I would be infinitely more comfortable with a battle plan. "Lennox. We should have—" I paused when I noticed him staring at me. "Why are you looking at me like that?"

He grinned. "I'm going to kiss you now."

I swallowed hard. "Ohhh-kay."

"You're okay with that, right?"

I nodded. Except, I was freaking out because what if in the harsh light of day I didn't measure up or something? *Stop overthinking this.* Squaring my shoulders, I said, "Yup, go ahead. Do your worst."

"I'll have you know that it's my best. Just so we're clear."

"If you say so."

"I *do* say so," he said with a low chuckle.

"Let's do it."

He walked up to me, slow and sure, and then leaned down with a smile before his lips met mine. "Just so you know, from our peripheral vision, everyone is staring."

Heat lit my cheeks, but I wasn't going to be deterred. I tilted my chin up and kissed him back. When he pulled away, he took my hand and gestured towards the blanket. "I got you something."

My cheeks were still enflamed, and I tried not to look around to see who might have noticed, because frankly, I didn't really care what they thought for the most part. "You got me a present? You didn't have to."

He laughed. "I know I didn't have to, but I wanted to. That's the point."

I ducked my head. I didn't have the heart to tell him that usually the things most guys got girls, I was not into at all. He pulled out a box that looked about the size of something like a necklace, and I was worried. I didn't like necklaces. They interfered too much. They were easy to catch on things. But if he gave me a necklace, I would wear that necklace every damn day.

His laugh was low. "Don't look so worried. Just open it."

I plastered a wide smile on my face, hoping that just this once I could lie. And lie well, because I didn't want his feelings hurt. Nonetheless, I opened the box. And then my heart skipped. "Oh my god."

He grinned. "Do you like it?"

I grinned so wide my cheeks started to hurt, and he stared at me. "Do you have any idea what you look like when you smile?"

I tried to control it, but there was no stopping that grin.

"No."

"You have the most amazing dimple. It's really cute. You look adorable. And stunning, and beautiful, and you know what, I'm glad you don't smile more often. Otherwise, somebody else would have noticed. This way, I can keep you all to myself."

"You're ridiculous, but thank you." Nestled in the velvet of the box, was an ornate switch blade. When I lifted it, I tested it on my finger. Perfectly balanced. Outstanding craftsmanship. And on the hilt of it was what looked like a fairy. "This is amazing. Thank you."

"You are welcome. Now, I did get this information that a lot of couples carve their names into this tree, so we're going to carve our names on it."

"I had no idea you were so cheesy."

He grinned. "Just call me cheese master. Now, hand it over. Let the man get to work."

I frowned at him as he took the knife. He was holding it wrong. He was going to hurt himself. I watched him as he found a patch on the bark and started to try to etch. I was worried with the way he was using it. I gently put my hand on his shoulder and said, "Why don't you hand it over?"

"No, I can do this."

I laughed. "No, I know you can. I'm just saying that maybe you let someone who handles a knife regularly do this."

He looked at his etching and frowned. And then he nodded. "Yeah, good point."

With a grin, I took the knife from him, and then resumed what he'd started to carve. I etched our initials onto the side of the tree, and then I stepped back and smiled.

He whistled low. "Well, I'm glad I let you do that because what I was doing was not going to work."

I glanced up at him. "Thank you for this. I didn't—" How the hell did I explain to him that I never thought I'd be *that* girl. To have someone like this. Someone who made me feel fluttery and light. Who saw me for who I really was. There was too much to say, so instead, I said, "This is the best day."

I switched the knife again and placed it back in its box and into my backpack. Lennox pulled me to him as we sat under the tree, then pulled out earphones for the both of us. "So, why don't you explain to me about why the hell you used to kiss Rhys?"

I laughed. "Haven't we been over this? It's really been eating at you, hasn't it? Are you worried that I've been crawling through Rhys's bedroom window too?"

He smirked. "I know for a fact you would never sneak into Rhys's room. You don't trust him. Unless, of course, you're holding onto his throat. You don't trust him as far as you can throw him."

I shook my head. "You'd be right about that."

The smirk softened into something happier. Warmer. "So I know I'm the one you trust," he said quietly. "Which for me is the best of all."

I could barely look at him when he was smiling like that. "Why do you see me so clearly?" I whispered.

The answer seemed to be easy for him.

"I've always seen you clearly, Sloane Lauder."

CHAPTER EIGHTEEN

SLOANE

THE WEEK WAS like a dream. A dream I'd never dared to have, because I'd hate myself for wanting it. Wanting the boy who'd made my life hell since ninth grade.

But he was so much more than that, wasn't he? He was so much more than his sharp edges— he was full of love for his sister, he was a loyal friend, he was obsessed with making my body limp with pleasure.

He was obsessed with my smile.

Every night I snuck into his dorm room, and every night we kissed until we couldn't breathe, until the only thing we could do was touch and touch and touch, until we were both shivery and sated.

The first night we did this, I thought maybe we'd finally have sex, that maybe we'd finish what we'd started in the maze. But when we were kissing in his bed, and I asked him if he had a condom, he'd stared down at me with his gorgeous golden eyes and said simply, "Not yet."

"What do you mean, not yet?" I'd whined, taking his hand and pushing it into my panties so he could feel how wet I was. "I want it now."

"But I want it perfect," he'd insisted. "You deserve better than a bloody dorm bed, Sloane. Give me some credit. Besides, if all this pussy needs is to come, then I know something that might help . . ."

And then he'd disappeared beneath the blankets, all gold eyes and wicked grins, and then I was too distracted to protest about anything.

So yes, the week was a dream. Of his hot kisses and greedy touches, of walking together through the halls, of knowing our initials were carved into the school tree, of being *his*.

But it was a dream threaded through with a nightmare—because between every kiss, between every lick of his tongue or slide of his fingers—the truth lurked.

I'd spied on him. For the one person Lennox could never forgive.

I'd spied and stolen, and even if I hadn't given the letter over to my father, I'd still given him everything else. I'd still *taken* the letter when I had no right to, and I still hadn't told Lennox that I did.

I'd still treated Lennox like he was his father, when his father was all he'd ever tried *not* to be.

✧　✧　✧

"EARTH TO SLOANE," Cash Constantine said. I looked up from where I'd been staring at my wrapped hands. I needed to unwrap them, I needed to shower and pretend to go to bed so I could sneak into Lennox's room, but my father had texted an hour ago and it was all I could think about.

> **Dad:** lmk if you see anything new from our friend. from our original friend too.

He wanted more on Lennox. More on Cash too, although I didn't know how many ways I could tell my father Cash was no more involved with trafficked antiquities than he was involved with competitive pie eating.

I still wanted to catch criminals when I was older, I still wanted this life, but god, I didn't want to investigate my friends. My boyfriend.

I wanted even less to lie to my boyfriend, which was what I was doing every day I didn't confess.

"I'm here," I said to Cash, offering him a weak smile. "Just thinking."

"Well, I'm always here if you want to talk," he offered hopefully, his eyes dropping to my mouth.

"I don't talk," I reminded him, unwinding my hand wraps.

"I know," he said with a swallow, his eyes still on my mouth. "But, uh, if you wanted to. I could be there. Listen. Shoulder to cry on and all that."

I wound the hand wraps into neat bundles and fixed him with a look. "Do I look like the type of girl who needs a shoulder to cry on?"

"Well, no. But maybe you're the type of girl who needs someone who'd help her bury a body? I could do that too. The Constantines aren't always as up-and-up as they claim to be, you know. I could maybe help destroy some evidence for you?"

That did make me smile again. "Maybe you do know me after all, Cash." I tossed my hand wraps in my bag and stood. "And thank you. It's just parent problems."

And Lennox problems.

"I definitely know all about those," Cash said. "Anytime you need me, Sloane. I'm serious."

"Same to you," I said with a nod. And then I

went back to my dorm to shower.

That night passed as they all have—with Lennox licking my pussy until I came against his mouth and then me passing out in his arms—but the next day did *not* pass as it should have. I emerged from my last class to find Lennox leaning against the wall opposite my classroom door, a smug, evil smile on his face.

"You're coming with me, my sweet, vicious darling. We have plans."

LENNOX WAS A prince.

I forgot that sometimes, when it was just us in his bed, just his fingers inside me and his raunchy murmurs in my ear; I forgot that he had the kind of money and influence someone like me would never fully understand.

And so when I followed Lennox outside— thinking he'd planned another autumn picnic for me or something—I was led not to the lawn or the woods, but to his family's waiting Maybach, where a bag of my things had already been stashed in the trunk and my coat was waiting on the seat, folded neater than any coat should be.

"It's all arranged with the school," Lennox had said as he'd handed me into the car. "They think you're visiting your father."

"What do you mean? What's been arranged?"

"You're mine for the weekend, Sloane Lauder." He'd given me a look that sent goose-bumps popping all down my arms and legs. "All mine."

And so now here we were in New York City, in a hotel so expensive and glamorous that of course it belonged to the Constantine family. We were whisked through a soaring, Beaux Arts lobby by a private butler, who also saw us up to our room and shepherded in a lavish dinner served on embarrassingly fine china before he left us to eat and explore.

"Come eat," Lennox said as I wandered over to the window nearest the food-laden table. "I promise it's not fairy food, you won't be bound to me forever if you eat it."

He almost sounded sad about that when he said it, but when I turned to look at him, there was only his usual mocking smile, the one that looked so unfairly good on him.

"Sloane," he prompted after I turned back to the window. "Come."

"I can see Central Park from here," I said to him. "And so much of the city too. And these rooms . . ."

I pivoted on my heel as I gestured to the sumptuous suite around us. It was done up in dark wood floors and soft gray walls, hung with silk brocades and upholstered in leathers and velvets. Beyond the dining room, a four-poster bed waited in a bedroom the size of some apartments. It was in the very center of the room, like an altar of fluffy pillows and Egyptian cotton.

"Why are we here, Lennox? Why did you bring me here?"

He got up from his chair and prowled over to me, his smile fading into something darker. Hungrier.

"Guess."

You deserve better than a bloody dorm bed, Sloane.

"We're going to have sex here," I said, not as a question, but as a statement.

"Yes, we are," Lennox replied, sliding his hands over my hips and down my legs. I was still in my Pembroke skirt, and so he was able to ruck up the fabric and grab handfuls of my ass, squeezing the flesh there until I gasped and dropped my head on his shoulder.

He kneaded my bottom as he whispered in my ear. "Always with these sensible knickers, my little virgin. It's like you know how much they fucking turn me on. Because you don't mean to get me hard, do you? You don't mean to make me crazy. But just *seeing* you makes me crazy. And now that I know how soft this pussy is, how wet it gets for me, I can't even think when you're around. I can't even think when you're *not* around. My mind is just filled with you and when I can see you again. When I can touch your cunt again."

He moved from kneading my ass to pushing his fingers down the front of my panties. I slumped in his arms as he found the swollen bud of my clit and started rubbing.

"So yes, darling girl, we are going to have sex tonight, and tomorrow night. I'm going to make you as crazy as you make me. I'm going to make you as obsessed with me as I am with you, so that you can't think, can't breathe, can't even *exist* because wanting me is that excruciating."

His clever fingers moved down even farther, and he nudged my boots apart with his handmade Italian brogues to spread my legs.

"Fuck, you're so wet," he groaned, pushing his fingers inside me. "How are you already so wet?"

I bit his neck in response, right above his uniform shirt collar, and he groaned again.

"Forget the food," he breathed. "I have to

fuck you now. Tell me you're ready. Tell me you want it."

I grabbed his hand and pushed his fingers deeper. "I want it." God help me, I wanted it. Even though we'd hated each other. Even though I'd spied on him. Even though I was pretty sure I was falling in love with him and it might be the worst mistake of my life.

I wanted it.

I lifted my face for a kiss, and he obliged me immediately, his lips firm and hot on mine, wasting no time before they demanded I part for his tongue. And then he stroked inside my mouth with it, kissing me like I belonged to him, kissing me like he'd caught me and now he would claim his prize.

And when I opened my eyes as we kissed, I saw that his were already open, heavy-lidded and sultry, like a lion watching his next meal.

Lust kicked me in the clit; my belly was a bottomless well of want. All I wanted was him, was his erection deep inside me. I wanted him to fuck me so hard it felt like fighting. I wanted us to tear each other apart until we were both sated and wet and spent.

"Lennox," I murmured, moving my mouth to his jaw, to his throat. "I don't want to wait." My hands went to his belt; they were shaking as I tried to work it open, that's how needy I was. "Right now, let's do it right now. Right now, please—"

He was half-laughing, half-groaning as I finally managed to get his belt open. "Let's at least go to the bed—you deserve—"

"We've nearly fucked on a rugby field and in a maze and in a cold-ass *scullery*, I'm not a princess or a shrinking violet. Goddammit, Lennox, just put me out of my misery."

His cock jumped in my hands as I freed it from his uniform trousers, and pre-come was already beading at the tip. "I think you've got it wrong who's been more miserable," he growled and then he spun me around. "Hands on the fucking window, Sloane. Stick that pretty arse out. Present yourself for me."

I obeyed, letting out a shuddering breath as he flipped my skirt up over my ass and tugged my panties down to the floor. I heard the tear of a condom, and a low, ragged breath as he rolled it over his length, and then his fingers were back at my slit again, smearing my wetness all over.

"It should be like this," he said hoarsely, fitting his wide crown to my narrow opening. "It should be exactly like this. In our uniforms. Dirty and urgent. Just like I've been stroking myself thinking about for years."

My head dropped forward against the cool glass of the window. "If I'd known . . ."

"We would have both failed out of Pembroke, wouldn't we? We would have never left our rooms. We would have been fucking every chance we got."

"We still hated each other then," I pointed out, my breath hitching as he pushed the head of his cock inside me.

"That would have made it all the more fun," he purred, giving me a small stroke. Just that plush crown going in and out. "Think of the scratches you would have left on me. Think of the handprints I would have left on your tight little bottom."

I was barely breathing now. "Lennox . . ."

He kept going with his magnificently dirty words, giving me another toe-curling nudge of his thick cock. "Think of how you would have pinned my wrists to the floor and took what you wanted until I couldn't give you any more. Think of how fun it would have been to have me between your legs and not know if I was going to tongue-fuck you or bite you or both."

"Are you saying that we're not going to do

that now?"

"You want me to fuck you like I hate you? Because I'll happily oblige, my cruel temptress. I may not hate you, but you can bet everything you own that I still hate how much I want you."

I lifted my head enough to look over my shoulder at him. He'd taken off his uniform blazer when we got to the room, so it was just him in his shirt and uniform tie, with the sleeves rolled up and the tie loosened. His white-blond hair fell onto his forehead, and his sharp, beautiful features looked sharper than ever in the low, ambient light of the hotel room.

"I hate how much I want you too," I admitted in a whisper. "It's a weakness."

"Then it will be a weakness we share."

And for some reason, that felt like the most romantic thing he could have said. He wasn't promising me forever, he wasn't promising me eternal devotion. He was telling me that we would suffer this sickness for each other together. That we were both in this, and that we would try to survive it together instead of separately.

And if my traitorous heart ached for more—if my mind warned me that I was in real danger of loving Lennox Lincoln-Ward—then I ignored them. I would take Lennox with a blindfold and my ears stopped up, that's how much I needed him with me and in me.

He leaned forward, not to kiss me, but to bite the back of my neck. "I'm there, Sloane, can you feel it? I can feel it. Right fucking there." He nudged his hips a little to prove his point, showing me exactly where the resistance was just inside my channel. "I'm the first man inside you. The first you'll ever have. Almost like you saved yourself for me. Almost like you knew you were supposed to."

"Oh, is that right?" I challenged, but my breathless squirming belied my words.

"Yes, that's right. You were mine from the moment I saw you. I would have killed anyone who touched you, who got to know what your cunt felt like before I did. Who got to know exactly how you liked to be rubbed . . ." His fingers followed his words, finding my sensitive spot at the top of my seam, and caressing it expertly, sending tremors all down my legs.

"Lennox," I murmured. "Please . . ."

"Breathe in, sweetheart," he said, and I breathed in. At that moment he bit my neck again right as his hips punched up—right past my virginity.

The pain from his bite was the perfect distraction from the pain between my legs, but I cried out all the same, crumpling against the window as Lennox bottomed out inside me.

I was used to pain—both the pain of being struck in sparring and the sore muscles that came from sparring—but this was something different. Something deeper and sharper. But there was no escaping it, no recoiling away, because I was still impaled on him, I was still caught between his lean but powerful frame and the window.

He kissed my neck and stroked my hip under my skirt. "Stay still, my little sprite, and I'll make it better." His fingers resumed their strumming on my clit, sending confusing signals of pleasure to compete with the pain of his invasion, and then he started talking, and my body melted at his words.

"You're so fucking tight, Sloane, just like I knew you would be. So narrow you can barely take me, can you? And it feels so good in here, it feels so hot all around my cock, I don't think I can ever leave. I don't think I can ever stop fucking you. I want my entire life to be fucking you . . ."

Abruptly, and I didn't know how because his thick erection between my legs was still taking my breath away, I came against his fingers. My knees buckled and my entire body shook as I screamed out his name against the glass.

And that seemed to be the last straw for his control. All of a sudden he was gone, no longer inside me, and then I was being scooped up and carried into the bedroom.

"I feel like a princess," I said dazedly as he placed me on the giant fairy tale bed.

"Well, I *am* a prince," he said, yanking off his tie and unbuttoning his shirt. "Just say the word if you need me to make things more princess-y."

I watched him strip off his shirt, revealing etched muscles and a line of golden hair arrowing down from his navel. I parted my legs and raised up my skirt so he could see my wet cunt as he undressed, and his gold eyes practically scorched me into ash.

"On second thought, I've been told I have more of a *fairy assassin who fucks* vibe," I said as he crawled onto the bed. His wet, latex-covered cock jutted lewdly from his uniform pants as he did. He was like having my own personal pornography.

"I'll take the fucking literally," Lennox said, covering my body with his own and then entering me with one rough thrust.

I arched against him, running my hands up

his back, grabbing at his shoulders and arms. He braced himself on his hands and stared down at me with a raw animalism that took my breath away. All that muscle, all that power, all that unfiltered will—all of it was bent towards fucking me. To claiming me. As if this was the inevitable outcome after all these years, and the insane thing was that I welcomed it, I wanted it, I was claiming him right back. Scratching his back like he said I would, writhing underneath him as my second orgasm built and built.

And as I panted his name and shivered through my climax, as he gave me several deep, bed-rattling thrusts as his own orgasm tore through him, I decided I didn't want to know if this was still revenge for him. I didn't want to know if part of him still hated me, if all of him still hated my father, if I was the tawdry means to a bitter end. I didn't want to know, because somehow, against my better judgement, I'd fallen for him. I'd fallen in love.

Fuck me.

Chapter Nineteen

Lennox

I NEVER SLEPT better than when a well-pleasured Sloane Lauder was snuggled in my arms. There was something about someone so strong, someone so fierce and yet so remote, trusting you enough to sleep in your embrace. And that it was *this* girl, the one I'd known was mine since the moment I saw her . . .

Well. It made my cock hard and my chest feel strange. The usual Sloane problem.

I woke her up that morning with slow, wet kisses between her legs, knowing she was sore and would need to be eased into more fucking. But there *would* be more fucking, if she'd let me. Whatever tender feelings were growing for Sloane were still indelibly tied to my need to possess her, for her to belong to me, and *those* feelings were indelibly tied to my cock.

And after she came, we ate a leisurely break-fast and then went for a walk around Central Park to enjoy the last of the leaves. And when we came back, I had a surprise all ready for her.

"Oh, Lennox," I heard her say as she walked into the bedroom and then caught sight of the bathtub in the doorway beyond. "Jesus, I'm so cold and that looks so good right now."

I was smiling as I came up behind her. Steam curled off the surface of the bath I'd arranged for us while we were gone. Champagne chilled nearby, and fresh rose petals drifted on top of the water, subtly scenting the air. "That's the idea, darling."

Sloane turned and gave me a look like I'd just moved a mountain for her. "You did this?"

"What better way to warm up after a bracing stroll in the cold autumn air?"

She nearly smiled, catching her lower lip with her teeth just in time to stop it. "You shouldn't have."

I was obsessed with her smile, obsessed with seeing it as much as possible. "On that, dear ferocious one, we shall have to disagree," I said as I pulled her lower lip free of her teeth with my thumb. "Now, let's get you naked."

An arched eyebrow. "Ah, so there's an ulterior

motive."

"You doubted that there was?" I asked as I unwound her scarf and unbuttoned her coat. I tossed both on the bed, and then started on her clothes—a black turtleneck and leggings, along with her boots—and she let me undress her with a small sigh.

"I guess I don't mind. If you didn't have an ulterior motive for this afternoon, then I would have."

"That's what I like to hear."

Once I had her naked, I took my time looking at her. At her small, high breasts, at her flat stomach and narrow hips. Her arms were sculpted with elegant curves of muscle, as were her thighs and calves, and between those firm thighs was a triangle of dark, silky curls that I knew would smell like honeysuckle if I buried my nose in them like I did this morning.

"Fuck, you're gorgeous," I murmured, already hard against the placket of my trousers.

She blushed. "Thanks."

"I mean it, Sloane. Feel me."

She reached out and wrapped her strong, slender fingers around me through my trousers, and we both made a noise. I'd never been this horny, never needed to fuck *so goddamn much*, but with Sloane, I felt insatiable, like an animal in rut. I needed to fuck her more than I needed my next meal or swallow of air.

"Get in the bath," I breathed. "Wait for me with your legs open."

She squeezed me—hard. "I'm not an obedient girl," she murmured. "But luckily for you, I also happen to want to wait for you in the bath with my legs open."

And then she sauntered off, her firm arse swaying hypnotically as she did.

I undressed in record time, flinging my clothes everywhere, and striding into the bathroom to find her not only with her legs open, but with her fingers in between her thighs, petting herself.

"Bleeding Christ," I choked, staggering to the edge of the bathtub. "Are you trying to kill me?"

She laughed—and there! There was that fucking smile! Lighting up her entire fucking face like the sun. Just seeing it made me want to fall to my knees and worship her forever, but I settled for a long, urgent kiss that left her gasping and then climbing into the water behind her. I hauled her into my lap, so that my hard cock nestled against her arse, and then I helped her lean back against my chest, so that her head rested on my shoulder and I could see all the way down her front, from her wet breasts to her parted thighs.

I found a tightly pointed nipple and started teasing it under the water. "Are you warmed up yet?"

"Not yet," Sloane murmured. "I think you'll have to help."

"Hmm, like this?" I covered her tits with my hands and plumped them, kneaded them, until she was breathing hard in my lap. "Does that help?"

"Yes," she said. "Oh god, yes. Oh, Lennox." She took my hand from her breast and molded it over her hot mound. Her seam was slick with more than water, and I played there, running my fingertips back and forth.

"You're amazing, you're so good at that, I love when you touch me," she was confessing, all in a dreamy, lustful chatter. "I wish you could kiss me forever; I wish I lived in your bed; I wish I'd known you earlier."

"We've known each other for years," I said, biting her earlobe as I circled her clit with my fingers.

"*Really* known you. Known how loyal you are and perceptive you are. How smart and thought-ful and kind. Known how much I would lo—"

She stiffened in my arms, cutting herself off, and suddenly my heart was pounding against my chest, as if it was trying to crack my rib cage open and slither out to meet her. As if my life depended on what she was about say.

"Sloane?" I said hoarsely. "Known how much you would what?"

She hesitated. "How much I would like you," she finally said, and it felt like my heart had fallen flat out of my body and gone down the bathtub drain, that's how disappointed I was. That's how much I wanted her to have said something else. Another word.

She tried to change the subject, I could tell. "I started birth control at the beginning of this week," she said. "Just in case. And I trust you, Lennox, I trust that you're clean."

She had my complete attention then. "Are you saying you'll let me inside without a condom?"

"Yeah," she said, wriggling her bottom against me. "I am."

My cock jerked so hard against her that she laughed again, but I was past laughter, past everything but hunger and need. I lifted her higher against my chest and then reached under her to fist myself. "Right now, Sloane. Right fucking now. Work yourself down on me," I said. "Make it so I'm splitting you open."

I'd fucked so many girls before now, but fucking Sloane was ruining me for anyone else. Because watching her slender, athletic frame arch and shiver and flex as she slowly impaled herself on my thick cock made me realize I only wanted to fuck strong girls. Lethal girls. Girls who could choke me out as soon as make me come. It was something about those sleek muscles maybe, or about that deadly grace as she moved. About knowing she was strong enough to take everything I had to give her—which was a lot. Which was so much it scared even me.

And then there was the fact that my cock was entering her tight hole without anything between my skin and hers. I'd never fucked raw before, and feeling the silky clasp directly on my dick was excruciating, pure hellish bliss. I needed to come right away, I needed to pump her full of my seed so she could finally *see*, finally *feel*, how she'd destroyed me and made me her thrall. Maybe I was a prince on paper, but I would be a pauper for Sloane and her tight, velvet cunt in a heartbeat.

She finally took all of me, her tight backside flush against my lap as her thighs spread on the outside of my mine. And then she leaned back against me as I started playing with her tits again, breathing hard, because the effort of not coming right away was almost too much.

"You feel like every dream I've ever had," she murmured up to me, raising her chest up to my roaming hands. "Like every fantasy I ever wanted."

"God, you are so fucking sweet when I'm inside you," I groaned, squeezing her tits and biting at her neck. "Ride me, Sloane. Use that little assassin's body of yours and make yourself come on me."

She did. God, she did, her thighs and her arse flexing deliciously as she sat up and started screwing me, started moving in small figure eights. Water dripped off the slick, flat muscles of her back and trailed down the furrow of her spine, and right below the water, I could see the twin dimples at the small of her back, dimples made for my thumbs as I wrapped my hands around her hips.

She looked back at me over her shoulder, and her green eyes were filled with more than lust, more than need. They were filled with that word she hadn't been able to say, the word I wanted her so desperately to say. And I knew then as she started to come, her eyes still on mine, that I'd been lying to myself since the maze. Since long before the maze.

This wasn't revenge.

This was something scarier and more dangerous to us both. And when my stomach tensed and my balls tightened and I started throbbing my climax into her pussy, I knew what it was. Because I trusted her. I *liked* her. I wanted her in my life not just now, but after Pembroke, after college. Forever.

She was mine, I'd known that for four years, but now I knew the truth.

I was hers.

I loved her.

CHAPTER TWENTY

LENNOX

I WAS A sap. It was all right. I knew it.

Coming back from the city, and I still couldn't let go of Sloane's hand. Even at her door, when she opened it and turned around with a smile on her face, all I wanted to do was keep holding her hand, stand there, and just be with her.

You've gone soft, mate.

"This is me." There was a smile in her eyes as they danced.

"I guess it is."

She inclined her head back towards the open doorway. "Well, I'm going to go in now."

But still she made no move to step inside. No move to take her hand from mine. I leaned against the wall, next to the door jamb. "I really don't want to let you go."

Her lips twitched. "I really don't want to be let go."

I knew she had things to do. On the way back she'd mentioned her economics exam she needed to prep for. *Don't be that bloke. Let her go so she can be great.* I leaned forward and pressed a soft kiss to her lips. "Are you okay though?"

The smile that touched her lips was shy. "Yeah, I'm okay. I mean, I'm sore in places I didn't know I *could* be sore, but it's a good sore."

I shook my head. "Oh, Sloane, what am I going to do with you?"

"What? I'm just saying."

What she was saying was good for my ego, but I still didn't let her go. "So what are the chances that you might want to sneak into my room again? I mean, at another time, obviously, when you are not quite so sore. And after you've studied." God, I was an arsehole. She'd just told me she was sore. I'd kept her naked basically all weekend.

Not to mention, she might want a break from me. She might be tired of me already.

She laughed but pulled her hand free of mine. "Well, I have some homework to do, and I need to make headway on econ, but maybe when I'm done, if you don't have any homework to do, we can 'not do' homework, together." Her smile was sly.

And just like that she gave me hope. "Sounds like a date." I kissed her again. This time I lingered, savoring every flavor on her lips, because I knew it would have to tide me over until I could see her again.

Which would be in probably several hours. God, several hours without her.

Get it together.

I could do this. I wasn't a complete pussy. I was, however, a bloke with a girlfriend now. So that was new. I pressed one more kiss to her lips, and then I let her go. I already felt cold and sought her out again and gave her another. One that held more promise, but then promptly let her go. This was becoming a problem. "Oh my god, why can't I stay away from you?"

"Why don't I want you to?"

"Sloane, you're killing me. Okay, let's take care of business, okay? I'll see you after."

"I'll text you when I'm done," she promised. "And then I will head over there."

"It's a date."

I forced myself to walk away. And as it was, I walked briskly. Down the hall, down the stairs, across the landing, up the other set of stairs through the boys' corridor, and then down the hall to my room. It was the only way. Otherwise, I was going to stay, or ask her to come study in my room. If she did that, there is no way in hell she would ever get anything done. Nor I.

Once I got to my room, I grabbed my laptop from my desk and plopped on the bed to get something done. But a stack of papers fell with it. With a groan, I knelt to pick them up, leaving my gaze eye level with my desk.

I frowned when I saw the fateful letter just sitting there.

That was not where I'd left it before. I never left that out. It—and everything like it—always went into the file cabinet. Christ, *especially* this one.

This one was a letter to Nicholas. After all, he was my little brother, my father's love child with Graciella, currently being raised by his grandparents in Cyprus. I wouldn't have just left this out for anyone to find. And then an unpleasant memory surfaced.

One with Sloane, when I'd caught her in my room, standing *right next* to my desk.

No, mate, don't jump to conclusions, steady on.

The problem was, even as my brain tried to work out any viable reason she would have to be snooping, I couldn't come up with one, so I sent her a quick text.

> **Lennox:** *I changed my mind. Can you come here for a minute?*

The little dots jumped and her reply was quick.

> **Sloane:** *I still have econ to study for . . .*
> **Lennox:** *I promise, I'll be quick.*
> **Sloane:** *I feel like I've heard these words before. It can't be quick.*

Despite my current mood, my cock twitched. Because she was right. I couldn't be quick.

> **Lennox:** *It's important.*
> **Sloane:** *I'll be right there.*

She arrived in less than three minutes. Concern was written on her face. "What's the matter?"

The letter burnt a hole in my hand. I knew I had to ask her. In my body, in my soul, I felt like I already knew the answer, but I needed her to tell me. "This letter, have you read it?"

Her face, that beautiful elf-like face with the delicate features and her beautiful eyes, told me everything I needed to know about the truth in that moment. But I still needed her words. I needed to complete the process of her breaking my heart.

"I can explain," she whispered.

I blinked at her and then sank down on my bed. "You can bloody *explain*?"

Sloane ran a hand through her soft chin-length hair. "Look, I know. It was a huge breach of trust and downright pathetic of me, but you should know that when I took it, our relationship was nothing yet. We hated each other. And my father, he'd asked for some information, I didn't know what to do then. I couldn't refuse him, so I did it. Now that I know you, and now that we've—"

I put a hand up to stop her talking. "Your *father*?"

She paled. "Lennox, I'm so sorry."

Sorry.

She had torn through my tender, fledgling trust of her, she had searched through my life without seeking any context, she had found the one thing in here that I'd poured the most of my heart into and planned to deliver it to my father . . . and she was *sorry*.

You know fucking what?

I was sorry too.

"Even if I could accept that you didn't know

me before when you came into my room and read something that wasn't yours, before you pretended to care about me, the fact that you're trying to suggest you did it for your father makes me not want to believe a word you've said."

She started to shake. "Lennox, I *do* care about you. I didn't then. Admittedly, we were on opposite sides."

"And what about after?"

"I just—I'm sorry."

Her words were ineffectual, because how could you just say sorry? How could you just overlook the pain and think it could be okay. Sorry didn't even begin to cut it. "Your father. You know what your father did to my family. You know, and you still broke in here to spy for him." My voice stayed low, stayed cold.

Even though everything inside me felt shredded and raw and hot.

She started to stutter. "I—look, I know. I didn't expect these feelings. And I thought you hated me. And that's no excuse. I wanted to tell you. Especially after I knew you, I wished I hadn't done it. I wish I had just told him no, but he knew the one thing that would get me to give in to his request, so I did it. But I want you to know that even though I broke your trust, I didn't tell him about that letter. I just gave him the information on the computer."

I couldn't breathe. In the place where my heart had been, something mangled and pulpy gave a sharp, sudden lurch. "My computer?"

She swallowed hard. "I know I messed up."

"What did your father want? It must've been something big for you to offer your virginity to me for it, right? So what was he after?"

She shivered at my cruel words, and I hated myself for caring, I hated myself for even noticing. She'd done this. She'd done this to us.

Not me.

Sloane swallowed, and I could see her doing the math if she should tell me the truth or not.

I sighed and made it sound bored, the way I usually do. The way I pretended with other people, people who didn't know me and never would. "Let me just make this simple for you. There's nothing you can say that would make me care about you ever again, so you might as well tell me the truth. What would make you do this to me . . . to us?"

Her beautiful face went from a flushed pink to stark chalk. "I guess there were some murmurings that your father had left accounts unreported and the government is still trying to recover those.

Yours and Aurora's accounts were untouchable, because you were minors, and you had trusts which were given by your grandparents. My father thought that maybe you and your trust could lead them to the money, or maybe you had access to the accounts that your dad had left behind. He wanted me to do research and see if I could find it."

"So your father asked you to fuck me and get access to my accounts?"

She flinched as if I'd slapped her. "No. He didn't. He asked me for information before I fell for you. Up until two weeks ago, I thought you hated me. Besides, I would never do that. Us getting together had nothing to do with my father."

Was she daft? "You can see how I don't believe you, right?"

Tears shimmered in her gaze, and I almost relented. I wanted to forgive her.

I wanted to pull her into my arms and tell her that while I was angry, I couldn't give her up.

I also wanted to throttle her, legitimately watch as the light went out of her eyes. It was better if I didn't touch her.

"I know, Lennox. I'm really sorry. I just—I did it because it was my father. He's all I have . . .

all I've had for so long, and all I'd ever wanted was to be like him. But not anymore, and if I could go back in time, I would."

"Well, too bad there's no such thing as a time machine. At least I know what I'm dealing with now. You can go."

She reached for me. "But Lennox—"

I forced my face into a mask, wiped it blank of any pain that I felt, because then she would *see* too much. "I said you can fucking go. I have nothing to say to you. We're done. You know what, I was bothered by that idea of you and Rhys because he would have ruined you. But as it turned out you're just like him. You're a devil in disguise. You deserve someone like that."

She stepped toward me. "Lennox. I just—"

For a moment, I let the mask drop. Just enough that she could see my anger, every sharp blade of it. So she could see exactly what I thought of her fucking lies, her fucked-up excuses.

"What part of *leave* didn't you understand?"

It didn't matter that every part of my soul was on fire. It didn't matter that I just wanted to hold her and believe her explanations. None of that mattered, because she cut me deeper than my father ever could.

Or hers.

"Lennox, I didn't tell him about who you were writing to. I didn't tell him about the letter."

"I don't believe you. Now get out."

I marched to the door, yanked it open, and waited for her to go through it. I was done. Done caring. Done obsessing over her. I was just done.

Chapter Twenty-One

Sloane

THIS WAS MY fault. I knew it was my fault. What I hadn't expected was quite this level of pain.

What, you weren't ever going to tell him?

Maybe I hadn't planned on telling him. What the hell did that say about me? I'd allowed myself to get so caught up in Lennox Lincoln-Ward wanting *me* that I forgot the simple basic tenet of being me. I believed in truth and justice, and I had wronged him.

There was no point in crying about it. No point wallowing in the pain like I had been for the last week. I had made my own bed. I had done this to myself.

Of course he no longer trusted me. Of course he no longer wanted to be with me. It was the predictable result and consequence of my own actions.

You are an idiot. Did you really think this would last?

Why hadn't I asked my father for more information? Why hadn't I simply said no to the old man?

At the end of the day, I was responsible. Even though I should not have been participating in missions. And more importantly, it had felt wrong at the time, and I'd still done it because my father had asked me to. I'd still done it because I wanted to impress him so badly that I was willing to forget who I was.

I wasn't above stealing something from a room. I wasn't above giving someone their comeuppance. I wasn't above a little revenge. Hell, I thrived on it, had built my reputation here at Pembroke on it, but I was always, always honest. And I hadn't been honest with Lennox. I had hurt him, however unintentionally.

This was the outcome. An outcome I'd created for myself.

Serafina stepped into the room, clearly surprised to find me not curled up in a ball as I had been most of the week. Sure, I'd gone to classes. But outside of those classes, and doing the bare minimum I had to for school, I hadn't done much else other than lie in bed and cry.

I just hadn't thought it could hurt so much. That feeling of disappointing someone. That feeling of someone no longer wanting you. That loneliness I'd felt since my mother died, it was nothing compared to now. Nothing compared to the rejection I'd felt from someone I cared about.

He didn't reject you. He simply walked away from a damaging situation . . .

Lennox had been the only person besides Sera, Aurora, and Tannith to really see me and care about me as a whole, and I'd ruined that. I had hurt him. No wonder he'd rejected me. But while I might not be able to fix us, while he might never forgive me, at the very least, I could make it right.

I could get my father off his tail, to stop investigating him and his family. If my father wanted information on the Lincoln-Wards, he was, A, going to have to get it himself, or B, going to have to let me go. Lennox and Aurora, they hadn't done anything wrong. They were just boarding-school kids—the ones parents pawned off to the Ivy League pipeline as soon as they could hold a pencil—like I was. And if the agency couldn't see that, then did I really want to go to work for people like that?

"Okay, so you look like maybe you'll be eating today?"

I gave Serafina a wan smile. "I have eaten, and I showered. And I've been to class. Happy now, Mom?"

She lifted a brow. "As my grandmamma used to say, don't sass me." Her words dripped with an added southern drawl. Her grandmother on her father's side of the family had come from New Orleans. The old battle-axe held up a damn long time. And Sera had spent quite a few summers with her before she passed. So every now and again, she had these random southern utterances intertwined with her van Doren cultured inflections.

"Sorry, I didn't mean to sass you, Mama Sera, I'm just saying, I've done all the things you always ask about. Showered. Ate. Class. Homework."

"Oh, well I see you're feeling better."

"Not really. But it's possibly time for me to stop wallowing. I messed up, but now I have to deal with it head on."

"I know, babes. But how are you going to fix it though?"

"That letter I stole along with the files on Lennox's computer, I'm going to use it to show my father that Lennox isn't working for his dad. I want to show him that Lennox is a good person.

If he can see that, maybe he'll stop the witch hunt."

Sera folded her arms as she plopped onto her bed. "Do you think that will work?"

I shrugged. "I don't know. I did a lot of damage. And maybe he shouldn't ever trust me again. I might not be able to fix us, fix what I did, but I can get my dad off his tail. At the very least, I can do that."

She levelled her gaze on me. "Sloane, can I say something?"

I sighed. "What?"

"Know that this is coming from a place of love. And I love you a lot."

"Stop sugar coating and just tell me."

"Honey, are you in love?"

I blinked at her. "I don't understand the question."

With a soft laugh, she shook her head. "Right, I get you. Of course, you don't. It's just, yeah, you messed up. Everyone messes up. And I know you, your whole thing about honesty and forthrightness. You will do everything in your power to correct it. You just have that *crusade* look about your face. Like you cannot sleep until you fix it. And honey, that's a love kind of thing. The way you've been carrying on with this not sleeping, not eating zombie version of Sloane. Hell, as far as I know, bad guys could have broken in here this week and you would have let them."

I rolled my eyes. "I would not. I would have snapped out of it to kick ass, then gone back to bed."

She laughed then. "Okay, probably. But my point is, it's okay if you love him. And if you're going to talk to him, maybe you start with that."

I frowned. "I honestly don't even know if he'll accept that. I tried to, but he wouldn't give me a chance. And honestly I didn't deserve one. I really messed up. Really, really, really messed up. So maybe I deserve this. And the least I can do is put it right. This isn't about love."

"Uh huh. Well you said you were sorry. But sometimes, you have to go deep within the apology to show someone that you really, really care about them, more than just you're sorry for hurting them. But that because you care so much, it never would be intentional. And he doesn't know that. He thinks you're the same Sloane who has always loathed and despised him."

I frowned. "I never loathed or despised him. *He* has always been the one who loathed and despised me. He was just a guy I stayed away from. The guy whose radar I tried to stay off of.

But somehow he was always there, always messing with me."

Sera rolled her eyes. "And why do you think that was?"

I shrugged. "I don't know."

"Sloane! Lennox Lincoln-Ward has loved you since the moment he saw you. He, just like every other idiotic male mammal of our species, had no idea how to say that. And so, he pulled your pigtails and tortured you. Because he's a man, he couldn't just say, 'Hey, you've given me pants feelings. I don't want pants feelings when I think about you because maybe you're not what I pictured for myself. But still, *pants feelings.*"

I choked in a laugh. "Oh my god, did you just say pants feelings?"

She nodded. "Yep, pants feelings. Because, accurate."

"Yeah okay. I'll start with pants feelings."

She laughed. "Or you could say, 'I love you and I'm sorry.'"

I mulled over what she said. She had a point. If I told him how I felt instead of just saying 'I'm sorry. It's hard to explain,' he might be willing to listen.

I stared at my laptop then. At the very least, maybe if I apologized better and got my father off his back, at least he wouldn't hate me so much.

"You may have a point there, Sera."

"What? Me have a point? Honey, do I have to remind you, I'm never wrong?"

I laughed. An actual genuine laugh for the first time in a week.

"Hey, one chuckle, I'll take it. Better than the grunts and head nods I've gotten all week."

As Sera got busy doing homework and tapping away on her computer, I was closing up my research. I finally found the address that Lennox had been writing that letter to. I thought it was in reference to the lawyer or something, but it wasn't. The address I found was for a little boy about seven years old, living with an elderly couple in Cyprus. They were Graciella de Marco's parents, but despite them having the same dark hair and olive skin as Graciella, the school picture of Nicholas I found showed a little boy with white blond hair and bright gold eyes.

Lennox hadn't been writing to a lawyer. He'd been writing to a little boy. A little boy, who like him, had lost his father. Lennox was his only protection from the world.

That little boy was Lennox's half-brother.

CHAPTER TWENTY-TWO

LENNOX

"YOU WOULD THINK after you're finally getting laid by the girl you've been obsessed with since you got here, you'd be in *much* better spirits. But no, you're still in a shit mood. Maybe I should have fucked her first. Tested the roads. I wouldn't have fucked it up."

I pushed away from the ledge along the roof on top of the dorms—a spot we came up to when the weather was decent—and walked towards my friend. I was going to kill Rhys tonight. Throw him right off. I gave zero shits.

But Owen and Keaton were there, and even Phineas made a move to stop us. And Phineas was a shit starter. He loved to watch and see if things would actually come to blows. But after the last time, I think he saw that we were really going to kill each other if allowed.

Rhys fought against Phin's hold. "No, let me go. He wants to pop me, and he thinks he can. He's welcome to give it a go. It's not my fault he's a pussy. I'd primed the girl for him. I'm the world's best wingman, brought him the girl he's been mooning over for ages. *Ages*, mind you. And I let him have her. But he fucked it up. And she's a fantastic kisser."

"You don't know what the hell you're talking about," I ground out.

Owen kept his arms wrapped around me. "Keaton, Phin, get him the fuck out of here. This isn't helping right now."

I thought Rhys was going to fight the command, but Keaton was already approaching him with crossed arms and a grumpy expression. Rhys could fight all he wanted, but when Keaton said it's time to go, it was time to go. And there was no fighting him. The fucker was too big.

On our way back downstairs, Owen pinned me with a glare. "Seriously, what the hell is wrong with you?"

I grumbled. "Nothing."

"Look, I get it. You and Sloane had some kind of dust up, but you've been in this mood for over a week. Time to snap out of it. If you don't like her anymore, great, fine, you don't like her. But this has to stop. You almost threw Phin *into a fire* last week. And with Rhys, you'd both end up bloody if this shit goes on for much longer."

Just Rhys's reminder that I could no longer feel her lips on mine sent a pang of pain through my body. She'd betrayed me. The one person who I'd given my full trust to. How was I supposed to forget that? And why did it hurt so bad? I'd thought I'd insulated myself from it all, but Sloane had cut me deep.

Owen sighed as he took the spot next to me. "Look, I get it. You got beef with her old man. And him trying to spy on you and getting her to do it, that was fucked. But your beef is not with her. It's with the old guy. You're mad at the wrong person. You should be mad at *your* old man because he was the one who actually fucked up. He made a mess of your family. Not her father, not her. Your father. Sure, her old man was tenacious. Went after yours with everything. But her father didn't actually do anything wrong. He was doing his job. Her old man, I'm sorry to say, put a criminal behind bars. And that criminal happens to be related to you. It sucks. Utter bullshit. But he's the one who hurt you. You're punishing the wrong people."

My brain felt like it had been put through the

blender. Like I was walking on a tightrope of emotions and if I took one misstep, my soul was going to go through a meat grinder.

I hated him. I hated them all.

Are you sure about that?

The pain was too close to the surface. All my defenses, my ability to push the pain down. Sloane had chipped that all away, and now I was one raw nerve. The words tumbled out even before I was aware of talking. "He was a prick," I mumbled. "Lied. Cheated. Charmed us and bribed us with gifts and games and hugs whenever he felt us slipping from his grip. And that was just at home. Outside the home . . . he ruined people's lives and still . . ." I blinked away the stinging in my eyes. "I can't let it go."

Owen sighed. "Look, parents are complicated and shit. And it's okay if you're mad at him. But be mad at *him*. Be mad at the person who actually brought you this situation. Her father had a job to do. He did it. Did your family get hurt in the process? Absolutely. And it sucks. But again, he was doing his job. And that's not on *her*. And the Sloane I know wouldn't have just left you hanging out to dry."

"The Sloane I know wouldn't do that either. But she did, didn't she?"

"Because her father asked her to. He's her dad, man."

"She still chose him over me."

Owen's chuckle was harsh. "So, you're telling me that even if your old man called from prison, asked a favor, there isn't some small part of you that would be tempted to do it? It's your father, you idiot."

I ground my teeth together. "Whose side are you on anyway?"

"Yours, man. Always yours. But when you're fucking up, it's my job to tell you that. We're more than Hellfire Club, more than just a couple of dudes that went to school together. You are my best mate."

"I didn't mess up anything. She snuck into my room, *stole* information from me, and gave it to her father."

"Yes, but maybe ask her why. Any idiot who knows her knows how badly she wants to work with him. He's all she's got."

"She had me." Those three words slashed a gaping wound over my heart.

Owen shrugged. "Did you tell her that?"

I opened my mouth to argue, but then that little nagging voice from the inside needled me.

You didn't tell her how you felt. You shagged her

until you both couldn't walk. But you never once told her how you actually felt.

Not true. I'd given her the knife. She must know.

I didn't realize I'd said it out loud until Owen laughed. "Dude, she's a girl. Girls need the words."

"And you're such an expert?" I muttered.

The smile slid off Owen's face. "I know enough. At the very least, I know when something important is about to slip through your fingers."

"That's not my fucking fault, Owen. She chose her father over me."

"Don't you know her? That essay in English that first year, talking about a significant moment in your life, when she talked about when her mom died of cancer, leaving her just with the old man. I'm not really in for the feelings things, but that got me right in the heart area. When she talked about how her father was all she had left, and she would do anything to make him happy. Do you remember?"

I swallowed hard. I did remember. Not that I wanted to.

"Right. So if you remember, you can see how she would have done this. And she feels terrible. You're punishing her for something your father ultimately did. That's not cool. She can't go back in time and tell your father not to steal billions from a bunch of unsuspecting people. She can't go back in time to tell him not to have a mistress. She can't go back in time and undo all the layers of pain your dad caused. She can't go back in time and make her father not do his job. You're mad at the wrong person, man. Or maybe you could be mad at Rhys because he's a dick, but don't be mad at Sloane. That'll only hurt you."

"I don't need a therapy session."

Owen scoffed. "As if you could afford my rates. Look, idiot, you can choose to actually have what you want and see that you're fucking this up, or you can continue on this path and let it eat you. Your choice."

"Didn't she have a choice when she decided to spy on me for her father?"

"Yeah, she did. But that choice was between someone she cares about and someone she refers to as the only person that she has left. Was that even a choice?"

I was pretty certain I hated Owen in that moment. I hated him for being right about this. Sloane's father had asked her to do something, and even I knew she would do anything to make her father proud. Anything.

Fucking hell.

I hated it when Owen was right.

CHAPTER TWENTY-THREE

LENNOX

EVERYTHING INSIDE MY chest and my stomach still felt like it was in a blender, but there was something else now. I wouldn't dare call it hope, but it was *almost* like hope. Maybe it was even better. Maybe it was understanding.

Maybe it was forgiveness.

I tried her room and found only a glaring Serafina, who'd briskly informed me, "I'm not a secretary for idiot boys who fuck everything up," when I asked where Sloane was, and went back to painting her toenails before I could figure out a reply that wouldn't further irritate her. I tried the library, the gym, the track, everywhere Sloane would normally be, until the memory came to me of her strong fingers curled expertly over of the handle of the knife I gave her, and then I knew.

I ran straight for the tree, thankful that at least

it was warm enough for the grass to be dry and unfrozen, and slowed down at the far end of the quad once I saw her. She was sitting like I'd never seen her sit, not once, with her legs tucked to her chest and her head resting on her knees. Her hand was outstretched, idly tracing our initials where they'd been carved into the wood, and she looked so small and forlorn and sad that I wanted to rip something apart, I wanted to make something bleed.

Except that it was *my* fault she looked so forlorn and sad. It was my fault she was alone and curled up in a tiny ball. My fierce Sloane and what had I done? I'd dulled her sharp edges. I'd dimmed her burning glow.

All because I'd been blinded by my need for revenge, by my fury at her father. When really my fury was all about my own father. God, I'd been so colossally stupid.

I came up behind her, slow and quiet, trying to think of what I should say. Trying to think of the words I needed to make things right before she knew I was there.

But before I could even speak, she said, "Nicholas is your brother."

I shouldn't have been surprised that she knew I was there, she was the daughter of a former spy, but I still was. And I was impressed.

"How did you find out?" I asked, coming to sit in front of her.

"The address on the letter was a solid lead. It didn't take long to piece everything together once I realized Nicholas was only seven years old. And of course, there were the contents of the letter itself. I finally translated it. You want to meet him someday, but in the meantime, you're giving him all your money."

I shook my head. "Not all. I set up a small trust fund for him, and the rest of my trust fund is going into new, smaller funds to help the children of the people my father defrauded."

She was still gazing at the tree, her head turned away, but I could see the quick flutter of her eyelashes as she blinked. "Oh. The transactions. The lawyer."

"It's not strictly legal, you see," I explained. "The trust fund is designed to *hold* money, not for it to be split up and sent all over. My lawyer and I had to be very creative to make it happen, but I had no other option, Sloane. The alternative was just letting the wound my father made in the world fester, and I couldn't live with myself that way. He'd already humiliated my mom, gutted our family . . . the least I could do was try to help the other families he'd humiliated and gutted, you see."

She finally turned her head to look at me. She looked miserable, her green eyes dark and open. "God, Lennox, I'm so stupid. It was all to help people, wasn't it? All that money you were moving around, it was to make things right."

"I want to make things right with *you*," I told her softly. "I was so angry about the breach of trust that I didn't stop to ask myself why you might not have trusted me. I was so angry at being treated like my father that I didn't ask myself if I'd partially brought it on myself. I spent so long making myself the bad guy—*your* bad guy—that I hardly deserved the right to be aghast when you treated me like a villain."

"I talked to my father. About Nicholas. I told him that it seemed that the money was going towards your brother and not toward anything shady, and he agreed. And when I tell him about the other people you're helping . . . well, he's already backed off. And he'll stay backed off."

"I know," I said. And then I put my hand over hers where it still rested above our initials. What I was about to say next was so hard to say and yet when I said it, it felt so good I could cry. "I trust you, Sloane."

"How can you?" she asked thickly. "After what I've done?"

The answer was so easy. "Because I love you."

A tear spilled out of each moss-green eye, twin tracks running down her face.

I leaned forward to kiss them. And then I kissed her. Gently, without demanding anything, until she could speak again.

"I love you, Lennox," she whispered, "and I'm so sorry, so incredibly sorry. I shouldn't have invaded your privacy. I shouldn't have taken anything. I shouldn't have hid it from you after. We spent so long being enemies, so long in this fucked-up game of chess with each other, that when the game changed and we became something more, I didn't know what to do. I didn't know how to change with it."

"Me either," I told her. "But we can start now, can't we? Start our new game?" I flatten my hand over hers, pushing her palm against our initials hard enough that I knew she could feel them against her skin. "Because if the alternative is being without my violent little sweetheart, I don't think I can handle it."

Even though tears still spilled from underneath those long lashes, a smile tugged briefly at the corner of her mouth. "I'm not that violent."

"You dry-fucked me on the rugby field after tackling me and mounting me. You choked me while you did it."

The edge of her mouth tugged upward again. "You brought that on yourself."

"Then let me bring more of it on myself. I've spent the last four years making you miserable, so I think it's only fair that you torment *me* for the next four years. Maybe for a handful of decades on top of that, just to make extra sure I've paid my debt to you."

"And how should I torment you?" she asked.

"Well, the dry-fucking was nice," I said, and she giggled a little. She'd uncurled enough that I could pull her into my lap, and so I did, guiding her lithe legs to wrap around my hips. She was all lean muscle and black boots and soft lips. Her eyes were the color of my entire world. And the minute her core rested against my semi-erect cock, we both sucked in our breath. My shaft quickly grew hard as granite underneath her and she started rocking against it.

"Dry-fucking is all well and good, but I think the best revenge would be something a little more intense," she said, reaching between us. When I realized what she was doing, I groaned.

"Darling, people might see."

"My skirt will cover it."

"But—" It was too late. She had me out of my trousers, and she had her knickers tugged to the side, and then she was spearing her soft cunt with my erection, wiggling and squirming her way down to the root.

"Bloody Nora," I swore, dropping my head forward onto her shoulder. "How are you even tighter than I remember?"

"Does that mean that I'm succeeding in tormenting you?" she asked coyly, moving her hips in such a way that her heavenly pussy caressed my entire length. My testicles drew up tight, and already a knot of urgent tension was pulsing at the base of my spine. I was about to come.

"God," I rasped. "Yes."

"Good," she purred, her tears drying, her nipples visibly hard even through her uniform jumper. "I have a lot of torment to pay you back for."

"Please," I groaned. "Torment me forever. Make my life agony. As long as you're in it, I'll suffer anything. I'll give you anything. My mouth, my cock, my fingers."

"What about your heart?" she asked, stilling her movement in my lap to look into my face.

"My vicious darling, it's yours," I said, flattening her hand over my chest like I'd flattened it over our initials earlier. "It's been yours for four years. Since the moment I first heard your name."

And that glorious smile of hers bloomed across her face like a flower finally facing the sun. "Then I suppose I better take good care of it."

"I don't care if you stomp on it, as long as you know it's yours."

"And how long is it mine for?" she asked as she started to come.

I held her shuddering and pulsing in my lap, savoring each and every flutter of her body before I followed her over the edge. What started in hate, in revenge, in lust, was now the one good thing in my life that I would never, ever let go of. Even if it was still dirty as fuck.

But that was how we liked it.

"How does forever sound?"

Epilogue

Sloane

"IS IT COLD?" Lennox murmured evilly in my ear as he gave me a slow, deep thrust. "It looks a little cold."

"Fuck you," I gasped, my naked breasts pressed to his dorm window. Outside was a blizzard—a real New England blizzard that was flinging snow and ice everywhere—and behind me was a very delicious, very naked prince, using my pussy. All while my nipples ached with a wonderful agony I couldn't decide if I loved or hated.

The lights were off, so no one would be able to see us, especially not with the storm, but there was something exciting about being in front of the window. Of knowing anyone could look up and see Sloane Lauder, the pierced and booted badass, getting railed by her former bully and loving it.

"I thought *I* was supposed to be tormenting you," I managed to say.

"Oh but you are," he breathed. "Do you know what torment it is to have this silky pussy around me? What suffering it is to see my cock sliding in and out of your tight little hole? The affliction of knowing your nipples are rock hard? And don't forget your clit against my fingers right now—it's so swollen and ripe, and that's just pure pain to feel, my lovely. Pure pain knowing you're about to come all over me."

"Lennox, after I come, I want . . ." I cleared my throat. I could be brave. After all, I'd climbed dorm room walls for him. I'd risked my heart for him. I could say this thing I wanted. "I want you to fuck me somewhere else."

"Somewhere else? You don't want the window anymore?"

I gave him a look over my shoulder. "No, your highness. Somewhere *else*."

"Oh," he said, his beautiful face going blank with shock. "*Oh.*"

His cock throbbed inside my cunt; it clearly was on board.

"I know you have lube, and I want to try. I want—" I was shy about saying this too, but I made myself because it was important that he know. "I want you to have been everywhere. I want my entire body to know you. To have felt you everywhere."

He stilled, his head dropping onto my shoulder. I realized he was catching his breath, as if the idea of fucking my ass was too much and he was having troubling existing just knowing it was going to happen.

"Darling," he finally said. "Are you sure? We don't have to do this. If this is you trying to prove that you're some kind of sex assassin, then I already know that—"

"I'm sure," I said softly. "I want to do everything. And I know you'll make me feel good." Even when he thought he hated me, he still made me feel good. Like it's part of his genetic makeup, wired right into his very brain, that he has to make Sloane Lauder orgasm as many times a day as possible.

Lennox didn't answer me, only resumed his rough thrusts from earlier, and his exquisite handling of my clit. And within seconds, I was coming, keening, rocking back against him and arching against the cold glass at the same time. He let me use his erection as long as I needed, and it was only until I slumped back into his arms that he pulled free and carried me to the bed, where he settled me on my side.

I was still limp and boneless from my climax when I heard the click of the lube bottle and felt the cool slickness smeared over my tight entrance. He was generous with it, coating me inside and out, and then sliding a finger inside to make sure I was completely ready.

And when he decided I was, he knelt behind my ass while I stayed on my side, and he pressed the flared crown of his cock to my slick rim. "I've never done this," he confessed to me with a sheepish smile. "I guess that makes me a kind of virgin."

I smiled back, and I could see him melt. He always melted for my smile.

"I hear the first time hurts," I teased him. "Are you sure you're ready?"

"No," he said, but he pushed forward anyway.

The invasion was intense, scorching, like nothing I'd ever experienced. It *felt* obscene, utterly filthy, and even though I didn't know if I could come again, I felt the stirrings deep in my belly of another orgasm as he slowly wedged his cock deep inside my tightest hole.

"I—" His entire body was trembling as he pushed all the way in. The snowy light from outside made his hair silver and his eyes an unearthly platinum. His cheeks and jaw were as sharp as his gorgeous mouth was swollen from kissing, and the look on his face as he looked down at me. . . Like his entire life had been formed by fate for the sole purpose of meeting me and fucking me.

"Fuck. So . . . good. Tight. Fuuuuuck me. So tight."

I dropped my hand between my legs and rubbed myself, climaxing abruptly and hard, and even though he hadn't even moved, Lennox followed me over, the slick heat of my ass too much to stand. Every muscle in his stomach and thighs tensed, and then his cock jerked hard inside me, over and over again, flooding me with his come.

And then after several long, breathless, urgent pulses, we both went still.

He looked down at his erection still gloved in my body and then up to my face.

"Marry me," he said, and I laughed.

He didn't laugh though. He pulled free, took us both to the en suite shower for a quick clean, and then he put me in bed and climbed in. He pulled me into his chest. "I'm not having a laugh, Sloane. Marry me."

I tilted my head back to look at him. "We're

not even done with Pembroke yet," I said, thinking he must still be joking somehow. "We're way too young."

"Then we wait until we're not too young. But I said forever, Sloane, and I meant it. I need you to know that I meant it."

I stared up into his perfect face. My former tormentor, the sole source of my misery for years. I loved him so much it hurt.

"Yes," I said.

His arms tightened around me, but his face didn't change. "Say it again."

"*Yes*, Prince Lennox."

He swore and his mouth came down over mine, his tongue in my mouth and his cock already stiffening against my belly again.

"But we have to wait to actually marry until after college."

"Fine," he said in the way of someone prepared to argue the point at a later date.

"And we can't tell anyone we're engaged until we graduate Pembroke."

He sighed against my mouth. "*Fine*. But I'll be reminding you every day. Every hour. You are mine, my sweet, fierce darling, and I'm keeping you."

"I'm keeping you first." I smiled against our

kiss, and he swore again, rolling me onto my back and crawling over me, sliding into my still-slick body with no resistance.

"That fucking smile will be the end of me," he grunted, starting to rut. "But never stop. It's the way I want to go."

"Killed by my smile?"

"Tormented to death by it."

And then for the rest of the night, there were no more words. Only the best kinds of torments.

And smiles.

Thank you for reading!

We hope you loved Iris and Keaton romance. There are more books in the Hellfire Club for you to read right now! *They call him the Ice King...*

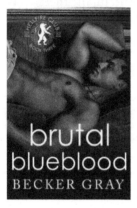

Owen Montgomery is arrogant and unfeeling—with cold, haughty manners and a British accent sharper than any knife. I've been secretly in love with him for years, knowing there's no way he could ever notice me. The scholarship girl. The poor girl. Until that night in Ibiza.

You can find BRUTAL BLUEBLOOD on Amazon, Barnes & Noble, Apple Books, Kobo and Google Play now.

Owen wants me, and he'll stop at nothing to have me. And soon I find myself with an impossible choice. Do I choose the future I always wanted for myself? Or do I choose the blueblood whose kisses are as brutal as his love?

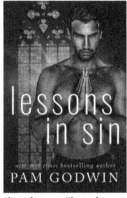

If you've already read Wicked Idol, be sure to check out LESSONS IN SIN. Keaton's youngest sister, Tinsley is in a different prep school… this one with a stern headteacher.

There's no absolution for the things I've done.

But I found a way to control my impulses.

I became a priest.

As Father Magnus Falke, I suppress my cravings. As the headteacher of a Catholic boarding school, I'm never tempted by a student.

Until Tinsley Constantine.

The bratty princess challenges my rules and awakens my dark nature. With each punishment I lash upon her, I want more. In my classroom, private rectory, and bent over my altar, I want all of her.

You can find LESSONS IN SIN on Amazon, Barnes & Noble, Apple Books, Kobo and Google

Play now.

> "LESSONS IN SIN is problematic, inappropriate, and blasphemously delicious. Pam Godwin writes unapologetically and from a place of primal desire. Enter all sinners."
>
> – CJ Roberts, New York Times and USA Today bestselling author of Captive in the Dark

The warring Morelli and Constantine families have enough bad blood to fill an ocean, and there are told by your favorite dangerous romance authors. See what books are available now and sign up to get notified about new releases here...
www.dangerouspress.com

About Midnight Dynasty

The warring Morelli and Constantine families have enough bad blood to fill an ocean, and their brand new stories will be told by your favorite dangerous romance authors.

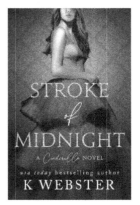

Meet Winston Constantine, the head of the Constantine family. He's used to people bowing to his will. Money can buy anything. And anyone. Including Ash Elliot, his new maid.

But love can have deadly consequences when it comes from a Constantine. At the stroke of midnight, that choice may be lost for both of them.

You can find STROKE OF MIDNIGHT on Amazon, Barnes & Noble, Apple Books, Kobo and Google Play now.

"Brilliant storytelling packed with a powerful emotional punch, it's been years since I've been so invested in a book. Erotic romance at its finest!"

– #1 New York Times bestselling author
Rachel Van Dyken

"Stroke of Midnight is by far the hottest book I've read in a very long time! Winston Constantine is a dirty talking alpha who makes no apologies for going after what he wants."

– USA Today bestselling author
Jenika Snow

Ready for more bad boys, more drama, and more heat? The Constantines have a resident fixer. The man they call when they need someone persuaded in a violent fashion. Ronan was danger and beauty, murder and mercy.

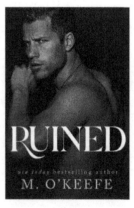

Outside a glittering party, I saw a man in the dark. I didn't know then that he was an assassin. A hit man. A mercenary. Ronan radiated danger and beauty. Mercy and mystery.

I wanted him, but I was already promised to another

man. Ronan might be the one who murdered him. But two warring families want my blood. I don't know where to turn.

In a mad world of luxury and secrets, he's the only one I can trust.

You can find RUINED on Amazon, Barnes & Noble, Apple Books, Kobo and Google Play now.

"M. O'Keefe brings her A-game in this sexy, complicated romance where you're left questioning if everything you thought was true while dying to get your hands on the next book!"

– New York Times bestselling author
K. Bromberg

"Powerful, sexy, and written like a dream, RUINED is the kind of book you wish you could read forever and ever. Ronan Byrne is my new romance addiction, and I'm already pining for more blue eyes and dirty deeds in the dark."

– USA Today Bestselling Author
Sierra Simone

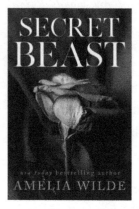

Get intimate with the Morellis in this breathtaking new series...

Leo Morelli is known as the Beast of Bishop's Landing for his cruelty. He'll get revenge on the Constantine family and make millions of dollars in the process. Even it means using an old man who dreams up wild inventions.

You can find SECRET BEAST on Amazon, Barnes & Noble, Apple Books, Kobo and Google Play now.

Haley Constantine will do anything to protect her father. Even trade her body for his life. The college student must spend thirty days with the ruthless billionaire. He'll make her earn her freedom in degrading ways, but in the end he needs her to set him free.

These series are now available for you to read! There are even more books and authors coming in the Midnight Dynasty world, so get started now...

SIGN UP FOR THE NEWSLETTER
www.dangerouspress.com

JOIN THE FACEBOOK GROUP HERE
www.dangerouspress.com/facebook

FOLLOW US ON INSTAGRAM
www.instagram.com/dangerouspress

Copyright

Made in United States
North Haven, CT
15 March 2022

17148421R00198